Also by Brian Farrey

The Secret of Dreadwillow Carse

The

COUNT[
CLOCKW[
HEART

The
COUNTER CLOCKWISE HEART

Brian Farrey

Algonquin Young Readers   2022

Published by
Algonquin Young Readers
an imprint of Algonquin Books of Chapel Hill
Post Office Box 2225
Chapel Hill, North Carolina 27515-2225

a division of
Workman Publishing
225 Varick Street
New York, New York 10014

LIBRARY OF CONGRESS CATALOGING-IN-PUBLICATION DATA

Names: Farrey, Brian, author.
Title: The counterclockwise heart / Brian Farrey.
Description: First edition. | Chapel Hill, North Carolina : Algonquin
Young Readers, 2022. | Audience: Ages 8–12. | Audience: Grades 4–6. |
Summary: "A prince and a mage must untangle the riddles from their
shared past to save the future of the empire—or risk seeing everything
they both love destroyed"—Provided by publisher.
Identifiers: LCCN 2021035432 | ISBN 9781616205065 (hardcover) |
ISBN 9781643752259 (ebook)
Subjects: CYAC: Princes—Fiction. | Magic—Fiction. | Ability—Fiction. |
Fantasy. | LCGFT: Fantasy fiction. | Novels.
Classification: LCC PZ7.1.F36935 Co 2021 | DDC [Fic]—dc23
LC record available at https://lccn.loc.gov/2021035432

10 9 8 7 6 5 4 3 2 1
First Edition

This book is dedicated to the memory
of my friend Ann Kaner-Roth.
Fiercely devoted in all things—
activism, friendship, marriage—but
nothing more so than as a mother.

TABLE OF CONTENTS

PART THREE

The
COUNTER
CLOCKWISE
HEART

PART ONE

1

The Boy Who Talked to Stone

It was the coldest winter morning ever on record in the empire of Rheinvelt when the people of Somber End awoke to find the Onyx Maiden in their tiny village.

The night before, they'd gone to bed, fireplaces blazing to ward off the bitter chill, safe in the knowledge that a statue of Rudolf Emmerich stood watch over the village center. Emmerich, Somber End's long-deceased first burgermeister, was a beloved figure in the town's history even to that very day.

So you can imagine the distress when dawn broke and the shivering residents scurried across the roundel in the village center on their way to work, only to find chunks of

Emmerich's statue everywhere. A hand here, a kneecap there. Clearly, there would be no repairing the venerated idol, as much of its considerable girth had been ground into dark-gray powder.

Where Rudolf Emmerich had once stood, gazing wistfully over the town he'd helped settle, something far less reassuring now held reign: As tall as a two-story house, a maiden made entirely of rough, dappled onyx loomed over the roundel. Adorned in armor, she appeared to be in the midst of a battle. Her right arm was thrown back, ready to strike with a cat-o'-nine-tails covered in rocky spikes. Her wild hair, blowing in an unseen gale, reached out in all directions, like a demonic compass rose. Most terrifying of all was her face—frozen in a permanent angry scream.

"Who could have done this?" some villagers murmured. The empire's most contentious neighbors, the mysterious denizens of the Hinterlands, were unlikely culprits. No one had ever seen these creatures (they were, again, mysterious). But the feral howls that rang out from the barren landscape to the west didn't come from anyone who might deliver an arguably symbolic statue.

"How could it just appear?" others asked. If the statue was the height of a house, it must have weighed twice as much. Moving it would have been tricky at best. Few ventured theories, because the most obvious answer—given the fate of the Emmerich statue—was that the Maiden had simply fallen from the sky.

Still other villagers asked a far wiser question: "Why did this happen?" These were the people who understood that sometimes whos and hows didn't amount to nearly as much importance as whys.

When the rulers of Rheinvelt, Imperatrix Dagmar and her wife, Empress Sabine, received news of the Maiden's mysterious appearance, they sent emissaries throughout the land, seeking answers. Master scholars pored over ancient tomes but found nothing. The Hierophants— keepers of the most mystical and arcane knowledge—had recently fled Rheinvelt, it was rumored, afraid to speak the terrible truths they knew. Soothsayers far and wide cast bones and consulted the ether. They all offered the same dire warning: One day, the Maiden would waken and bring a terrible reckoning. Not just to Somber End, but all throughout the empire.

This was too much. The villagers already lived under constant threat. The unseen inhabitants of the Hinterlands could attack at any moment (*mysterious*, many believed, meant dangerous). If (when?) an attack came, the people of Somber End would immediately be on the front line.

Perhaps worse was the fact that the Hexen Woods, home to a terrible sorceress known as the Nachtfrau, curved around the village's northern perimeter. It was said the Nachtfrau prowled the dreams of the villagers at night and would curse any who even *thought* of entering her forest. The statue's presence was one dormant threat too many. The people of Somber End wasted no time. Life came to a standstill as everyone in the village devoted themselves to a solitary task: getting rid of the Onyx Maiden.

Moving the statue proved impossible. A hundred horses with chained harnesses failed to budge the Maiden. It was like an invisible giant hand held her firmly in place. Attempts to destroy her proved equally futile. Anyone who took chisel to or in any way tried to damage the Maiden fell gravely ill for days or even weeks. And never once was a scratch made to her impervious stone visage.

Two months of solid scheming proved fruitless. The Onyx Maiden wasn't going anywhere.

Many people moved away to other towns in the vast empire, choosing to be as far from Somber End as possible to avoid the day when the Maiden finally awoke. Those who remained—most of them couldn't afford to move or had nowhere else to go—lived their lives walking on eggshells. No one knew what might rouse the Maiden from her troubled slumber.

Few, if any, mentioned what was only ever whispered. It was called the Coincidence, because no one wanted to believe it was more calculated than that. Ever since the

Maiden's arrival, Somber End's fortunes had taken a marked turn for the worse.

Crops failed. Cows gave half as much milk. Storms struck far more regularly and did much more damage. Fearful of the Maiden's wrath, neighboring towns refused to do business with what they believed to be a cursed village. Soon, those who'd stayed behind found themselves living in a dying town.

Then, one day, nearly six months after the Maiden first arrived, something curious happened. A poor, unassuming boy named Guntram Steinherz—only just turned eleven—went to the roundel and stared up into the Maiden's furious, cold eyes.

His parents had all but forgotten him. They were consumed with their own worries, often leaving their son to find his own way. Guntram fed himself. He kept the family's paltry fires stoked. He had no friends, so he was very lonely. Unable to bear the neglect, Guntram went to the statue, hoping she would rise up, eat him alive, and teach his parents and the children who mocked him a lesson.

But his desire to be eaten vanished once he met the Maiden's horrific gaze. Guntram was a boy whose blessing and curse was a powerful imagination. Where others saw ferocity in the statue's eyes, Guntram saw power. And at that first glance, he conjured a hundred stories in his head about how the Maiden had come to Somber End.

She was an enchantress whose spell had backfired, turning her to stone. She was a princess from a neighboring monarchy, fleeing from usurpers, whose only protection was to become a statue. She was the greatest achievement of a downtrodden mason who'd hoped the errant wish he'd made on a star would bring her to life to be his bride.

None of these stories explained the Maiden's terrifying countenance or warlike stance. That didn't matter to Guntram. He only knew she was powerful. And when she awakened, he didn't want to be her enemy. So he began talking to the Maiden.

Each day as the sun rose, Guntram would come to the roundel, sit cross-legged at the statue's base, and talk. He would tell the Maiden the history of Somber End. He would invent stories of ferocious warriors and fantastic creatures. At night, before bed, he told her his fears and dreams and hopes. He confessed how he hated his family's meager existence and how he longed to live in a castle with more money than he'd ever need. He ended each night by touching the base of the statue and promising, "I'll be back tomorrow."

And then, after a week of this, a second curious thing

happened. The crops started to grow again. The cows became bountiful. Storms turned to gentle rain. Traders who'd avoided the village returned to do business. Life became what it had once been under the watchful eye of the Emmerich statue. In fact, life became better.

No one knew how the boy had changed things. The more Guntram wove his stories, the more prosperous the town seemed to grow. The villagers soon called Guntram their guardian. Before long, people were coming from the farthest reaches of Rheinvelt to see the grotesque statue—and the boy who had tamed misfortune with his imagination.

Time passed, and that poor, unassuming boy grew into a tall, forthright man. After a decade spent talking each day to the Onyx Maiden, calming her imagined rage with stories and songs, Guntram drew the attention of the empress. The creatures in the Hinterlands had been growing more restless every day. Needing a wise and brave counselor, the empress summoned Guntram. He was given the title of Margrave and a place in her court. The new Margrave gratefully left Somber End at twenty-one years of age to get everything he'd ever wanted as advisor to the empire.

But Guntram, like a cog in a clock, is just a part of the story.

The springs and gears and coils of this story—its very heart—concern Alphonsus and Esme, two children whom the people of Rheinvelt would call saviors, who all would claim performed miraculous feats—and whom Guntram would try to kill.

2

The Barefoot Prince

On the very same day the Onyx Maiden mysteriously appeared in Somber End, Empress Sabine heard a voice in the imperial palace walls.

Sabine, it was said, was a woman with fire sewn into every stitch of her being. Remarkable in every way, the stout empress possessed an unquestionable wisdom, a staunchness of heart, and an unwavering compassion for all. She also had excellent hearing.

As the story goes, she was walking through the halls of the palace one morning, quietly making plans for an upcoming ball, when she heard a sound—as faint as the peeps of a robin hatchling discovering its nest for the first time. She scoured the palace, seeking the odd chirrup. When she entered the armory, she pressed her ear to the ancient walls and listened.

It was here. Just beyond the wall. And she could tell now that it wasn't a bird but the cooing of a human infant.

Some would have stopped to question how a baby had gotten into the walls. Sabine paused only to select the largest broadsword she could find. An extraordinarily strong woman, her powerful blows quickly loosened a large square stone from the mortar that had held it there for centuries.

Scant candlelight revealed a small shadow-stained room just beyond the wall. A room no one, as far as she could tell, had ever known about. Sabine groped into the darkness until her fingers grazed something cool and metallic. Clutching tightly, she pulled the unknown object into the armory.

It was a bassinet. Or it *wanted* to be one. Where most bassinets were woven from horsehair or wicker, this basket was made of tarnished iron sprockets, old skeleton keys, twisted brass coils the width of a child's arm, and broken hammerheads. A half-dome bonnet, crafted from a suit of armor's breastplate, shielded one end of the cradle. All as if cobbled together by someone who had no idea what a baby's bassinet should be.

Inside the basket, she found a small boy wrapped in a

threadbare gray blanket. His skin was a rich brown, the same as Sabine's—almost as if the two had always shared this connection. Stitched onto the blanket was a name: ALPHONSUS.

The empress immediately took baby and bassinet to the dining hall, where Imperatrix Dagmar was enjoying breakfast. The imperatrix nearly fell over when Sabine explained how she'd found the baby inside the armory walls.

"How long could he have been there?" the imperatrix asked. "Who put him there?"

"And why?" A font of sagacity, Sabine was known for asking important questions.

Dagmar was prepared to have the child sent to an orphanage. But her heart ached for her caring wife who'd clearly, in just minutes, fallen in love with Alphonsus. Dagmar knew that Sabine had always wanted a child. The imperatrix had not seen her wife this happy in a long time. She quickly agreed that they would raise the boy as their own.

That night, alone with the child in her bedchambers, the empress laid Alphonsus on her bed as she prepared him for sleep. Hoping to find a clue as to who might have placed the baby in the wall, Sabine examined every inch of the strange bassinet.

She tugged at the skeleton keys, fused together and

unmoving. She prodded at the hammerheads, twisted the gears, and strummed the coils with her fingertips. But nothing betrayed its origin.

She was about to give up when she ran her fingers along the underside of the bonnet. She felt small, fine grooves. Turning the basket over, she looked under the breastplate and saw these words etched into the metal:

> *When nights pass as hours the same*
> *The end of time will start*
> *A sacrifice is all that saves*
> *The counterclockwise heart*

Was it a nursery rhyme? It seemed very grim.

She puzzled over it until the baby started to cry. Sabine stroked the boy's face as she changed his clothes. Lifting his terrycloth nightshirt, she froze. There, in the center of his chest, was a clock.

It wasn't *on* his chest but embedded *in* it. The perfectly round, flat clock blended seamlessly with the boy's flesh. Ornate silver braids—the hour and minute hands—glistened against a black face and shiny white numbers. A thin strand of gold—the second hand—ticked away, keeping perfect time with a barely audible *brrda-tick, brrda-tick*. When she put her ear to the clock, the empress could hear the cogs and sprockets whirring inside where a heartbeat would otherwise live.

Was this what the rhyme referred to? No. This clock ran normally: clockwise. Still, she knew it was no coincidence. What had started as a curious nursery rhyme had quickly become a frightening portent.

The empress examined the boy carefully, gently squeezing his toes and rubbing his arms. She found no other signs of clockwork. With this one exception, he was a typical human child whose blood raced as fast as anyone's.

Sabine, who dearly loved her kind and benevolent wife, feared telling the imperatrix about this discovery. For while Dagmar was good-hearted, she was quick to fear things she didn't understand. And there was little to understand about a baby who had a clock in place of a heart.

The empress didn't need to understand the clock. She didn't even need to understand the ominous warning in the bassinet. All she knew was that any child callously banished behind a castle wall needed love. Standing there, hand to her chest, Sabine swore to give Alphonsus just that.

And so a proclamation went out, notifying all of the new royal heir. The palace was beset by gifts and good wishes. Fireworks laid siege to the night sky in celebration. Surely this was a good omen, meant to counter the appearance of an onyx maiden in Somber End.

The years flowed and, as any mother will testify, Alphonsus grew faster than Sabine wanted. Whereas another monarch of her stature might have handed Alphonsus over to a legion of governesses, the empress devoted herself to her son's upbringing. As he grew, she taught him about art and literature. She taught him mathematics and history. And whenever she could, Sabine taught him to indulge in his curiosity. Her own, she felt, had always served her well.

She did not teach him compassion and kindness. There was no need. From an early age, Alphonsus demonstrated a strong empathy beyond his years. If a lord's son fell and scraped his elbow while the two were playing in the castle, Alphonsus was the first at his friend's side, dressing the wound and offering assurances. When he heard the children at the orphanage in the faraway city of Glückstadt would not receive presents for the Silver Moon Festival, he used his princely allowance to buy gifts for every girl and boy.

Growing up, Alphonsus was loved by all: his parents, the servants in the palace, the people of the land. He was instantly recognizable by his thick black hair that sported a thumb-sized shock of white near his cowlick. His bright, inquisitive eyes softened even the most surly heart.

He became known as the Barefoot Prince, for his penchant to go anywhere (indoors or out) at anytime (winter or summer) with nothing on his feet. Most believed this was because of the boy's eagerness to explore. People pictured Alphonsus bounding out of bed each morning, just barely taking time to get dressed before running off to read in the library or play in the gardens with the children of the lords and ladies who kept apartments in the palace. Odds were, if you spotted the prince, he was wiggling his crooked toes, as he did whenever he was happy.

In truth, Alphonsus was often barefoot because the empress hid the prince's shoes. She feared him straying too far from the imperial grounds and thought him less likely to do so without footwear. She alone knew of the clock in the boy's chest. Keeping the prince close meant it would stay that way.

When Alphonsus turned six and was old enough to grow curious about his clock—and, indeed, he had learned that no one else had such a device—the empress took him up to the castle's tallest tower, where she kept the patchwork metal basket he'd come in.

"No one knows about this," Sabine said, lifting the

boy's shirt and placing her palm on the clockface. "And no one *can* know about it." For the first time, she told him the story of how she found him in the walls.

As his mother spoke, the prince examined the strange bassinet. It was ugly . . . but beautiful at the same time. His fingers poked at the curious words engraved on the bonnet.

"Hours? Sacrifice?" he asked. "What is this?"

Sensing fear in his voice, the empress waved his questions away. "It's an old nursery rhyme," she lied. "It has nothing to do with you."

When the boy continued to fixate on the words, she cupped his chin in her hand and pulled his gaze to hers. "You are a very special boy, Alphonsus. But you must hide this." She tapped his clock once more. "You can't even tell the imperatrix."

Alphonsus immediately forgot the rhyme. The idea of hiding something from his other mother—a woman who had only ever shown him love and kindness—alarmed the prince. "But why?"

"Not everyone is as curious as you are. Some people are happy with what they know. And when something they can't immediately understand enters their world, they sometimes act in ways you might not imagine. To keep you safe, we must make sure that only you and I know."

The boy used his finger to trace the edge of the clock. For the first time, he hated it. "Where did it come from?"

The empress smiled and stroked her son's hair. "Where it came from will never matter as much as where you take it."

Sabine pulled the boy in tight, and together, mother and son silently swore to keep this secret.

Years passed. On a stormy day just before the boy's ninth birthday, when the rains threatened to wash away every road and every house, Imperatrix Dagmar returned from a journey to the Outer Valleys, gravely ill. Alphonsus and Sabine stayed at the imperatrix's bedside every day for a month, until Dagmar died. Wife and son were grief-stricken. They wore black for a year. The empress turned important matters over to her most trusted advisors; she knew the empire would be safe in their hands. And neither prince nor empress left their bedchambers but for meals or to console each other.

Swarms of the empress's subjects lined the streets outside the palace each day, hoping to spot the Barefoot Prince in the gardens beyond the gates. This, they knew, would be a sign that the period of mourning had ended. But the ivy on the gates grew thicker and thicker with the passing months until the garden was hidden from sight.

On the first anniversary of Dagmar's death, the empress decided that life needed to resume. She had responsibilities to her people. And she had seen the toll her wife's death had taken on the prince, who spent his days and nights in a listless torpor. It was time to move on. One morning, she woke, looked hard and long in the mirror to steel herself, then personally went through the palace and took down the black shrouds that had draped the walls since Dagmar's passing.

But Alphonsus could not be so easily stirred. Mourning had stunted the prince's curiosity. While the empress returned her full attention to the matters of ruling the empire, Alphonsus languished in the castle halls. He hugged shadows, unable to meet anyone's eyes. He lurked in belfries and cloisters and other places bred for solitude. Where the prince had always been the first to welcome new residents, he was all but invisible the day his mother's new advisor—a young man named Guntram Steinherz—moved into the palace's southeast apartments.

Concerned for her son, the empress sought a way to reach through the veil of sorrow that had gripped him. She had to get him out of the castle, even if it meant risking that someone would learn about the clock. Just days after the boy's tenth birthday, the burgermeister of

Somber End stood before the empress in her throne room with a petition. As she listened carefully to the man's concerns, an idea formed in Sabine's head. She knew how to help Alphonsus.

That idea changed the course of the prince's life forever.

3

Quest of the Huntress

ALTHOUGH IT WASN'T CLEAR AT THE TIME, PRINCE Alphonsus changed profoundly the day his mother made him promise never to tell anyone about the clock in his chest. If he couldn't trust the imperatrix to accept him for who he was, who and what could Alphonsus trust? When the empress had held him tight, Alphonsus had vowed to keep the secret. But something curious had roiled about, prickling in his stomach. It wasn't sadness. It wasn't grief.

For the first time, Alphonsus felt limited.

All his life, he'd enjoyed unfettered access to anything. There was nothing he couldn't do. There was nothing he couldn't say. Until now. Now, when dealing with those who'd always treated him with kindness and affection, he peered deeply into their eyes, searching for the secret hatred they might have buried within. This made him afraid.

From that day on, Alphonsus was much more cautious. He stopped exploring. He very rarely played with the other children in the palace. He remained polite to all he saw but kept to himself. The curiosity his mother had worked so hard to encourage ceased to flow, replaced now with crippling fear.

Everyone saw the change. Sometimes, the servants commented on how sad it was that the prince's infectious joy had vanished. Many wanted to understand why. But Alphonsus was determined never to give the people who might fear him a reason to do so. Even if that meant being afraid of himself.

Since he was six, Alphonsus had kept the promise he'd made his mother not to tell anyone about the clock in his chest. For the three years that followed, it was his only secret.

But by the time he'd turned nine, Alphonsus had another secret. One of his very own.

The death of the imperatrix had affected him in ways he couldn't quite understand. To begin, something had happened to his clock since Dagmar's passing. It didn't sound the same. For as long as he could remember, when he lay in bed, Alphonsus was lulled to sleep by the faint but persistent *brrda-tick, brrda-tick*. But after Dagmar's funeral, the prince noticed an extra sound.

Brrda-tick-click, brrda-tick-click.

He'd ignored it the first few nights, thinking it was his imagination. Yet when the palace fell absolutely still, and he held his breath, he could definitely hear the difference.

Brrda-tick-click, brrda-tick-click.

His mother had said the imperatrix's death had broken her heart. Is that what was wrong with him as well? Had the clock broken?

If worries about his clock's new sound weren't enough, the prince had also found himself seized by waves of panic. He'd always understood dying as a concept. But he'd never before lost anyone. He feared losing someone again.

Alphonsus started to worry about what would happen to him if Empress Sabine died as well. Who would be his new parents? Would they be as accepting of the clock? These questions ate at his sleep, drew dark rings under his eyes, and pulled down on him like a heavy wool cloak. This, on top of the sorrow he felt, left room for little else in his once wildly excitable mind.

A month after Dagmar's funeral, the prince made a decision: he had to find out where he came from. He'd never been even the slightest bit curious before. He was quite happy with his parents. They had always been good to him.

But now, worrying about the prospects of his mother's death and the change to the rhythm of his clock, Alphonsus couldn't help but worry about his own life. What if the clock in his chest should stop? What if it needed repair? Because there was no one else like him, surely only the person who'd done this to him could possibly be of any assistance. He *had* to find that person. And he had only one idea how he might do that.

One night, Alphonsus went to the south wing of the palace to the apartments of Birgit Freund, the royal huntress whose unerring skills had kept the royal family well fed since the prince was a baby. For years, the huntress had proven herself as the imperial family's closest confidant. Unsure as he was about trusting anyone, Alphonsus placed all his hope in being able to rely on Birgit's discretion.

Birgit, who'd secluded herself to her chambers so she could mourn the imperatrix's passing in private, was surprised to see the prince.

"I need your help," Alphonsus whispered. Birgit stepped aside, allowing the prince to enter her rooms. He pressed the door shut, meeting the huntress's eyes as he did so.

Birgit immediately stood at attention. From the time Alphonsus had been a toddler, the huntress had been the boy's only teacher aside from Sabine. Twice a week for the last five years, she had taken the boy hunting up the mountainside. She had steadied his arms the first time he drew a bow. She had crawled side by side with him across all manner of terrain, teaching the art of tracking. Like everyone else, she loved the eager-eyed prince dearly and would do whatever he asked.

"I'm ready to serve, my liege," Birgit said, hand to heart.

"Somewhere in this land," the prince began, "there is a clockmaker of remarkable skill. If needed, this person could replace a human's beating heart with a clock, and that human would live."

Alphonsus kept his promise to his mother. He didn't say how he knew this for sure, and Birgit, a loyal servant to the family, knew better than to ask.

"I want you to find that clockmaker and bring them to me," the prince continued. "Take whatever you need to complete this task. Money from the royal coffers, the fastest horse in the stable. Anything. Search far and wide, and do not return until you are sure you have the one person who could do this. Tell no one." He took a deep breath. "Not even my mother."

For the first time ever, Alphonsus read doubt in her eyes. It was an unusual request, to be sure. At first, he thought the huntress might refuse. She might even go straight to the empress to alert her of his plan. Instead, Birgit dropped to one knee so she was eye to eye with the prince.

"Your Highness," Birgit said, "I am reluctant to leave, so soon after the imperatrix's death. I fear the Hinterland beasts will sense weakness in her absence and take advantage of Rheinvelt. I should stay here to serve in case of trouble."

But the disappointment on the prince's face struck her to the very core. She would have given anything to ease the boy's pain. So she continued. "But I will do as you command. I only ask one favor in return. Every night, in the tallest tower, hang two colored lanterns: blue and green, the royal standard. Wherever I am in the empire, I will turn my spyglass toward the palace to see if those lights are hanging. This will be your signal to me that all is well."

Alphonsus agreed. The next morning, the huntress set out as Alphonsus had directed, in search of that most deft clockmaker.

That had been a year ago.

Things had changed considerably in recent days. The empress had returned to the affairs of the monarchy at last. She'd been so preoccupied with her own mourning that she'd never noticed Birgit had gone.

Every evening, for the last year, Alphonsus had gone to the top of the tallest tower in the castle just before bed. He'd hung the twin lanterns as promised, letting Birgit know he was well. And every night, he'd worried about her. He knew her task would not be a simple one. And after a year, he worried more. He hadn't known her search would take this long.

It was here, atop the tallest tower at dusk on a warm summer's evening, where the empress found her son scanning the horizon with his spyglass.

"You come here every night," Empress Sabine said. "What do you hope to find?"

Alphonsus lowered his gaze. "Nothing. It helps me think."

"What do you think about?"

"The imperatrix," he lied.

The empress laid her hands on the boy's shoulders. "I miss her too. But the time has come for us both to watch over the empire, as the imperatix would have wanted us to."

"How do we do that?"

"Today, the burgermeister of Somber End came to court with a petition. The people in the village fear that the Onyx Maiden there will be unhappy that Guntram Steinherz has stopped speaking to her. They have asked that he return to resume his duties as guardian of the Maiden. But I have decided that *you* shall be the Maiden's new guardian."

The boy's breath caught in his throat. "Mother! No, I can't do that."

"I've given this much thought," the empress said. "You are to be emperor one day. Leaders must do great things. You will start by bringing the people of Somber End comfort."

Alphonsus protested again, but the empress raised her hand, instantly silencing him. He knew she wouldn't be swayed. Sabine bent over and kissed her son on the forehead. "Your new duties start in the morning," she said. Then she turned and descended the stairs leading down to the palace.

Alphonsus leaned against the turret wall, stupefied. For just a moment, he considered taking the lanterns down from the window. If Birgit really could see the tower no matter where she was in the empire, she would know he was upset and come to his aid. He needed to talk to her about this.

In the end, he decided her mission to find the clock-maker was more important. One way or another, he would handle this on his own.

4

The First Miracle

The next morning, a valet named Heinrich arrived in the prince's bedchambers to prepare the new guardian for the day ahead. Still sulking from the night before, Alphonsus refused the valet's assistance.

Heinrich presented a pair of fine leather boots with silver filigree braids up the sides. "A gift from your mother," he said.

But Alphonsus wouldn't put them on. To the people, he was the Barefoot Prince. If his duty was to bring them comfort, he needed to be that which they expected.

Also, he was still angry with his mother for making him do this.

The prince fumed as Heinrich escorted him to the

palace gates, where he found Guntram Steinherz and two imperial guards waiting just outside. He knew of the Margrave, the empress's new advisor, but had never met the young man. Guntram was tall and broad-shouldered, and his square jaw stuck out almost as much as the briar patch of black hair on his head.

"Your Highness," the Margrave said, bowing deeply. "The empress has asked me to escort you to Somber End for your first day. She thought I might be able to answer any questions you have."

Alphonsus glared at Guntram. It was *his* fault the prince was being forced to serve as the Maiden's new guardian. If Guntram had just stayed in Somber End, none of this would be happening. Wordlessly, he stepped around Guntram and trod down the path toward the village. The Margrave and the guards fell in step behind the prince.

As content as Alphonsus had been to lock himself away in the palace while he mourned, he had to admit it felt good to feel the soft soil of the country lane between his toes again. He'd missed running barefoot outside. The warm summer sun chipped away at his sullen mood with every step he took. For the first time in a long time, the fear that had shaped his life for years ebbed.

"You do your people a great service, Your Highness," Guntram said. "Your parents have always worked tirelessly to protect the empire. Now you are following their lead. There can be no greater honor than to keep the Maiden appeased. I should know."

Alphonsus bit his tongue to keep from scoffing. From what he'd been told, Guntram had spent the last ten years talking to a statue. There had never been any proof that Somber End's misfortunes were tied to the Maiden's arrival, nor any evidence that Guntram's talking had reversed those problems. The Maiden's former guardian was just a bit too smug for the prince's liking.

"If you'd like," Guntram continued, "I could tell you about my days—"

"I think I can figure out how to talk to a chunk of stone," Alphonsus said coolly. In fact, he'd already decided exactly what he was going to say. He would tell the Maiden exactly what he thought of being forced to talk to her from sunup to sundown each day.

Villagers lined the streets of Somber End. Word had spread quickly that the prince would be the Maiden's new guardian, and everyone had turned out to greet his arrival. Alphonsus blushed as a cheer rang out when he first stepped onto the village's stone-paved streets. He suddenly felt very embarrassed for sulking.

Whether or not he believed the stories of what might happen if the Maiden awakened, these were still his people. And they were relying on him.

Head high, Alphonsus smiled and nodded as Guntram guided him through the streets. People threw bouquets of heather and edelweiss in his path. The crowd parted as the prince and his escort came upon the roundel in the village center. The cheers and praise faded away to razor-edged silence as Alphonsus turned a corner and the Onyx Maiden came fully into view.

She was larger and more terrifying than he'd imagined.

Alphonsus gaped up at the Maiden in silent horror. She was not at all like any of the skillfully crafted statues he'd seen in the royal gardens. There was a savagery to these chisel scars, as if the unknown sculptor had borne a grudge against the onyx. Alphonsus knew the image would inspire nightmares for years to come.

The bravado he'd built up on the walk to Somber End abandoned him, and Alphonsus suddenly had no idea what to do.

"What should I say?" he asked the Margrave meekly.

A triumphant grin flitted across Guntram's lips. "I told her about my life. I told her about my dreams, what I wanted. You'll find that once you start, it can be hard to stop. At the end of the day, I would say, 'I'll be back tomorrow,' and I'd touch her base so she'd know it was true." Guntram leaned in close, his hot breath filling the prince's ear. "She can grant you what you want, you know. If you're patient."

Alphonsus thought it would be easy enough to describe his life. He wasn't convinced the Maiden was in any position to grant him his desires. But if it meant he'd have something to say, he would do as Guntram instructed.

The Margrave bowed. "I am to return to the palace." He pointed across the roundel, where the two guards stood watch. "They will bring you back at the end of the day. Good luck, Your Highness."

As much as Alphonsus had resented the Margrave's presence, he didn't want Guntram to leave. But he dismissed his escort with a curt nod, then sat cross-legged at the base of the statue. He stared up into its fierce eyes. It felt silly to talk about his life.

Alphonsus became uncomfortably aware that a crowd of villagers stood around the edge of the roundel, their eyes focused on him. He got the idea they were all holding their breath, waiting for him to speak. It made him sick to his stomach. He closed his eyes and blocked them all out.

Soon, all he could hear was the whirring of his clockwork heart. *Brrda-tick-click. Brrda-tick-click.* He thought of Birgit, out there in the world, trying to track down the mysterious clockmaker.

She can grant you what you want, you know.

Guntram's words echoed back to the prince. He opened his eyes and whispered, "Who am I? Where did I come from?"

A collective sigh of relief issued from the villagers. Alphonsus doubted they could hear him; they had only seen that he'd spoken. For them, that was all they wanted: someone to talk to the Maiden. Many moved away from the roundel, satisfied that a guardian was at work again. Only a few stayed to watch.

Something stirred in Alphonsus when he spoke these words to the Maiden. He'd never said them aloud. Doing so made them much, much more powerful. His desire to learn more about who he was suddenly filled him to bursting in a way he hadn't felt since sending Birgit on her mission.

Alphonsus continued speaking, slowly at first but more eagerly as time passed. He told the Maiden the story of how he was found in a strange basket in the palace walls. He told her how his mother hid his shoes and he held up his bare soles to show the Maiden how calloused his feet had become.

As Guntram had predicted, the prince soon found it difficult to stop speaking. Before long, he found himself revealing everything he could think of: his sadness at the imperatrix's death, his anger at his mother for forcing him to come here. A stopper had been removed, and it seemed like nothing inside him would remain.

And then he told her the secret.

He told her about the clock in his chest. In a slurry of frenzied whispers, he revealed that he had a clock in his chest and that he was terrified it would stop and that there would be nothing anyone could do to help him.

"I'm so, so scared," he said, his greatest truth coming out wrapped in his softest breath. "Will I ever not be scared?"

Nearby, someone cleared their throat. For the first time since he'd started talking, Alphonsus broke eye contact with the Maiden. The royal guards had drawn nearer. The prince noticed that the sun had started to set. He'd been talking all day.

The prince got to his feet. Only a handful of villagers remained near the roundel, some of them having spent the entire day watching him. Alphonsus was about to turn and leave when he remembered Guntram's instructions.

"I'll be back tomorrow," the prince said solemnly. He reached out and touched the base of the statue.

Flash!

A burst of white light filled the roundel. A spark jumped from the statue to meet the boy's finger. A jolt of raw power sent the prince flying backward. A thunderclap drowned out the screams and gasps of the villagers.

Alphonsus landed roughly on the paved street. Pain shot through his arms and legs. Eyes wide, he sat up as the royal guards ran to his aid. Villagers circled around the prince as the guards helped the boy to his feet.

"Are you injured, Prince Alphonsus?" someone from the crowd asked.

Alphonsus blinked and took a deep breath. The pain quickly left his body. With a weak smile, he shook his head.

"Look!"

He couldn't tell where the shout had come from. But everyone turned at once to gaze at the Maiden. More frenzied cries rang out. Alphonsus pushed his way through the throngs and stood before the statue again.

Her face was as fearsome as always. But her right arm, once raised as if ready to strike with the cat-o'-nine-tails in her hand, had been lowered. The arm now rested at the Maiden's side. She still gripped the flail's pommel, but its spiky tendrils coiled harmlessly on the ground as if they'd always been there.

"It's a miracle," a woman muttered. "The prince has brought a miracle to Somber End."

The cheers that had greeted him on his arrival that morning paled in comparison to the shouts that rattled the town when people found that the Maiden had lowered her weapon.

The royal guards stayed close to the prince, ushering him quickly out of town and onto the path back to the palace. All the way home, Alphonsus fought to understand what had happened. He could only barely remember the flash that had sent him flying.

Dazed and exhausted, the prince went straight to his room. He would tell his mother what had happened in the morning. Fingers shaking, he prepared for bed. Alphonsus undressed before the mirror, searching for signs that he'd been injured. The finger that had touched the statue was unburned. He saw no scrapes on his back where he'd struck the pavement. He seemed perfectly fine.

But he *felt* different.

It wasn't until he faced his reflection, full on, that the prince noticed something new.

The clock in his chest was running backward.

5

The Last Hierophant

THERE WAS MUCH CAPTAIN WALDHAR ZWEIG DIDN'T KNOW about his new scullery maid.

Not that it concerned him. He'd come across the pale-skinned lass on a dock in Kesselberg, a northern city in Rheinvelt near where the sea became the Blau River. He'd almost mistaken her for a lad, with her short, spiky red hair, leather tunic, and breeches. From the deck of his ship, Zweig had watched the girl move from slip to slip, seeking passage downstream to Schneegart from each of the ships in the dock.

In the end, only Zweig's ship was headed south. The captain almost laughed when the girl made her request. No, it wasn't a request.

"You will take me to Schneegart," the girl said, each word sliding from her lips like an ice floe.

A demand! And to make matters more laughable, she had no money to pay for the trip. Zweig didn't know whether to admire the girl's spunk or put her to the lash for her arrogance.

But a voice seemed to whisper in his ear that helping would be a charity. The captain, who'd never performed a charitable deed in his miserable life, suddenly felt compelled to strike a deal to let the girl work off the debt aboard his ship until they reached Schneegart, just three days from now. The girl agreed.

The captain had never bothered to learn his new servant's name. When he needed something, he merely called out "Girl" or "Lass." Or "Wench" when he had a pall of gin on his breath. It wasn't long before the girl had earned her keep. She would swab the deck from stem to stern before the crew had woken. She would shout instructions down from the crow's nest—"Hard to port!"—when her keen eyes spotted the small but violent whirlpools that pockmarked the river's most dangerous stretch. And she made a schnitzel dish with thick egg noodles and rich cream sauce that left the crew stuffed but begging for more.

There were times, after the second day of the trip, when the captain wondered if the girl might stay on longer. It was clear she had no family or home. Perhaps she would be just as happy to remain on board once they'd arrived at their port of call. And, the captain mused that last night, when the gin had taken his thoughts, if the girl couldn't be persuaded to stay, she could certainly be forced.

But if Zweig had paused even a moment to find out more about his scullery maid, he would have learned that the girl's name was Esme. He would have learned that Esme did indeed have loved ones who had seen to her protection. And the captain would have discovered that any attempts to make the girl do anything she did not want to do would be very, very foolish.

Esme, Captain Zweig would have learned, was the daughter of two powerful Hierophants, the ancient order of magic wielders who'd vanished from Rheinvelt under mysterious circumstances. And before she'd traveled from the faraway place her people had gone ten years earlier, the girl had been enchanted with a potent charm by the Hierophant Collective, the wise council who ruled the Hierophants. This magic would protect her from harm, ensuring that no one took advantage of Esme.

Yes, there was much that a few simple questions would have told Captain Zweig about his hardworking servant. Not the very least of which was: trying to kidnap the girl would be a fatal mistake.

At dusk on the third day, they docked in Schneegart, a small port town near the northern edge of the Hexen Woods. Believing her debt paid, Esme gathered her belongings and went on deck to disembark. There, she found the captain and the crew—who'd seen their own duties ease up thanks to the girl's hard work—blocking her exit.

At first, the captain argued that leaving the port city, as he knew the girl intended, would be dangerous. The nearby Hexen Woods, the captain informed Esme, were home to an evil sorceress. The girl would be safer if she stayed on and continued to serve the ship. When Esme gruffly declined, Captain Zweig ordered his crew to withdraw the gangplank.

As soon as it was impossible for her to leave the ship, the crew formed a circle around the girl and captain. Zweig thought he heard the girl mutter something that sounded like "You don't want to do this," but he ignored it. He also ignored the girl's knowing smirk. Maybe that was his biggest mistake.

When Zweig grabbed at the girl, the air around Esme came alive, as if filled with a thousand unseen blades, whirling in every direction. The strange, invisible forces that had silently followed the girl on her journey, bound to her by the Collective's charm, made short work of the captain.

Esme stood perfectly still as her undetectable allies dispatched any of the crew that hadn't the sense to throw themselves overboard. By the time it was over, the girl stood alone, her eyes raking over the light of the full moon as it glistened down on the fresh blood covering the deck of the ship.

Esme sighed. This hadn't been the first time since leaving home that something like this had happened. She told herself that the captain only had himself to blame. Calmly, the girl picked up the captain's money pouch from the deck, lowered the gangplank, and descended onto the nearby pier.

So, this is where I'm from, Esme thought as she moved through the stone-paved streets of the port city.

Not this exact town, of course, but Rheinvelt itself. So different from where she'd been raised. All her life, she'd known the ice-glazed fjords and endless winter of the North Lands, across the sea. It was summer here in Rheinvelt. The scent of pine trees, carried on the warm evening breeze, smelled different. Fresh and bold. To Esme, the odor was like life itself. Not at all like home.

She had been only two years old when the Hierophants fled the empire. She'd been raised on the story of their lives in Rheinvelt and their eventual exodus. Crafted into those tales were vivid descriptions of the beautiful, verdant forests that covered the mountains and the way sunlight lit the clear, glassy lakes afire during the summer. Magic, her father had once told her, had always worked better for them here in Rheinvelt. Esme could hardly wait to see if this was true.

As an acolyte, Esme had studied the arcane arts of the Hierophants since she was old enough to raise her finger and trace a sigil in the air. Intense and relentless training—overseen by their leaders, the Hierophant Collective itself—had defined every day of her childhood. Some claimed that Esme, at just twelve, had become as skilled as her teachers.

Esme believed this too. Those who did *not* claim Esme was as skilled as the Collective *did* claim that Esme was arrogant. The young Hierophant didn't care. She dismissed this as jealousy. And now that she was back in Rheinvelt, she would prove her mastery of magic by performing the task the Collective had set before her.

She should have been exhausted, but the excitement on the ship had set her heart racing. Still, she knew she needed rest for the journey ahead. She scoured the streets until she found an inn. Without thought to the late hour, she pounded on the door.

A moment later, the thin curtains over the window glowed as a candle passed by. Esme heard locks unlocking just before the door flew open. A wizened man stood in a flowing nightshirt and a nightcap. He squinted into the darkness until his eyes found the girl.

"I require a room for the night," Esme said, without even an apology for waking the innkeeper.

The innkeeper yawned, a gale of foul-smelling breath escaping from behind a graveyard of crooked gray teeth. He took one look at the girl, paused only the briefest of seconds, and said, "Of course, young mistress. You look weary. Come in, come in."

Esme stepped over the threshold as the man opened the door wider. Any other time, waking the innkeeper at such a late hour would have made him cranky. He might have balked at a girl so young requesting a room, perhaps even refused her outright. But Esme knew she'd have no such trouble here.

"And who are you, good lady? Where have you come from?" the innkeeper asked, opening the ledger where he recorded the names of his guests.

"Esme Faust," the girl answered quickly, almost as if the words had been yanked from her unwilling mouth. "I am a Hierophant from the North Lands, past the sea." She forced her lips to purse and silently hoped the answer would slake the tired innkeeper's curiosity.

"Strange," the innkeeper said with a grunt. "That

must make you the last one in Rheinvelt. I'd heard all the Hierophants left years ago. No one really knew why."

Don't ask me why, Esme commanded silently, over and over. She buried her nose in the innkeeper's ledger and quickly scrawled her name within. Then she pulled a handful of shiny coins from her new money pouch and laid them on the innkeeper's desk.

The innkeeper nodded absently and presented Esme with a small brass key. "Your room is at the top of the stairs, end of the hall on the right. Would you like to be woken in the morning? Where will you be going?"

In her head, Esme cursed. But her mouth said, "No, I'll wake on my own. I am traveling to the Hexen Woods."

This was the nature of the protective charm bestowed by the Collective. Indeed, the nature of all magic worked by the Hierophants. Give-and-take. A double-edged sword. Hierophants called it the Balance. Every spell's intended purpose came with . . . less desirable side effects. This particular enchantment made anyone with the means to help Esme on her journey eager to do so. In return, if they asked *any* questions, she had to answer truthfully and without pause. Esme had been lucky Zweig didn't ask questions. Or perhaps Zweig had been unlucky.

The innkeeper, while under the charm's thrall and filled with the desire to assist Esme, seemed suddenly wide awake. His bushy eyebrows gathered in a knot above his nose. "The Hexen Woods! You're mad, girl. What could you hope to find there?"

Esme groaned but answered. "I seek the sorceress known as the Nachtfrau."

The girl slung her pack over her shoulder and made for the stairs, hoping to end the conversation. But as her foot touched the first step, the innkeeper called out. "The sorceress is evil, girl. She's a blight on the land. What business do you have with one so dark?"

Esme turned, compelled by the power of the magical energies that protected her. She looked the innkeeper in the eye and spoke softly.

"I've been sent to kill her."

Were the innkeeper not influenced by the girl's protective charm, he might have wondered who the girl thought she was. He might have questioned how a twelve-year-old girl planned to kill a powerful sorceress. He might have questioned *why*. Instead, the innkeeper nodded once before returning to bed.

The young Hierophant climbed the stairs and retreated to her room. She flung herself onto the bed and traced a sigil in the air with her smallest finger. She whispered a cant—the name of the sigil—meant to ease her into sleep. The faint outline of the symbol glowed with a golden shimmer in midair for a moment before vanishing.

As magical rest took her, the girl awaited the familiar dreams—the ones where she saw her father dancing among columns of light that sprang from the frozen earth like fountains; the ones where the air overhead blazed with a litany of glowing magic sigils. These dreams came every time she used the sleep charm. They gave her solace.

Her last waking thought was one of surprise. The Collective's charm had allowed her to tell only half her story to the innkeeper. She'd been forced to admit her plans for the sorceress when they met face-to-face.

She hadn't been forced to mention that the Nachtfrau was her mother.

6

To Kill a Prince

THE APARTMENTS IN THE SOUTHEAST CORNER OF THE IMPE-rial palace, used by all the lords and ladies in residence, faced the mountains. Guntram Steinherz had been given the most spacious apartment on the third floor. Each morning, he stood on his balcony just so he could watch the sun rise between the distant hills. It took his breath away to see the clouds ignite with oranges and purples. He knew he would never, ever tire of seeing it.

But what Guntram loved most about the view—more than the mountains, more than the spectacular sunrises—was that he couldn't see Somber End. The dilapidated village only served to remind him of his humble upbringings, his wretched parents, and a past he would do anything to forget. His first night in the new apartment, he swore to himself that he'd never return to his hometown again.

Since coming to live in the palace as the empress's newest advisor, Guntram feared that he, a poor peasant from a provincial village, wouldn't be accepted. But the tale of how he'd bravely faced the Maiden for ten years, fending off her wrath with his stories, had impressed the royal court. The lords and ladies immediately drew the young man into their circles and made him feel like one of them.

The week that followed exceeded Guntram's most vivid dreams. He sat in the empress's court, offering advice on relations with neighboring monarchies. He ate from banquet tables longer than the high street in Somber End. His generous salary meant he could afford the finest clothes—velvet capes and custom-made boots. It was as if every dream he'd ever told the Maiden had come to life. He had everything he ever wanted.

But his overwhelming joy shattered when, at the end of that first week, he entered the throne room to find the burgermeister of Somber End in discussion with the empress.

"You must send Guntram back, Your Majesty," the burgermeister was saying. "The Maiden needs her guardian. No one sleeps at night. We are afraid that Guntram's absence will anger the Maiden and cause her to wake, as was foretold."

Guntram's blood went cold. He feared that the old man's pleas would convince Her Majesty to release the new Margrave from his new duties.

It was pure luck that the empress had the idea to send Prince Alphonsus to serve as the Maiden's guardian instead. And Guntram was only too eager to make sure that arrangement worked out.

"An excellent idea, Your Majesty," Guntram said, bounding into the throne room. "The prince is a perfect candidate. The Maiden's heard all my stories. I'm sure Prince Alphonsus has many of his own to tell. I would be happy to escort him there myself, answer any questions he might have."

This meant seeing Somber End one last time, but it was a small price to pay. So Guntram did as he promised and took the prince to the village. And to further ensure his safety, Guntram had filled the prince's mind with tales of how easy it was to appease the Maiden. Surely the boy would take to his new task, fervently believing the statue might one day make his dreams come true. When Guntram returned to the palace that evening, he felt secure again, certain his new life would continue without incident.

But he hadn't planned on Alphonsus performing his new duties so . . . thoroughly.

"And every day," the prince reported after his fourth visit to Somber End, "people fill the outskirts of the roundel just to watch me speak to the Maiden."

Each time the prince returned from the village, he immediately sought the first person he could find and relayed every detail of the day. Today, Guntram had been the first person Alphonsus had found as he walked the palace halls. The prince tailed the Margrave and launched into his story.

"Yes," Guntram said, barely able to mask his impatience with the boy's boasting. "They did that for me too. At the start. Given time, they'll lose interest, and it'll be just you and the Maiden. Once they think you're helping, you won't matter to them."

Alphonsus kept right on explaining everything that happened in Somber End.

As mentioned, Guntram was blessed and cursed with a powerful imagination. It was a blessing when he needed to tell fantastic tales and beguile a willing audience. But it was very much a curse when he was left to contemplate terrifying futures that he convinced himself were real.

Guntram, who'd never had much growing up in a poor family, lived in constant fear that he would lose everything he'd gained. He loved his beautiful apartments in the palace. He loved the wealth and power that came from his station. But perhaps more than anything—something he'd only just realized—he loved the adoration that had come from being the Maiden's guardian.

Now, though, the people of Somber End loved Alphonsus. And that love didn't stop at the village's borders. The lords and ladies of the palace chattered about the prince morning, noon, and night. If gossip was to be believed, news of the prince had spread across the entire empire overnight. A single word colored the lips of all who spoke of Alphonsus: "miracle."

That one word ate at Guntram from within. It scuttled around his chest like a beetle, with pincers that grew sharper at the word's every utterance.

Alphonsus continued to go, day after day. By all accounts, he sat as expected at the statue's base and whispered quietly. And even though the statue never moved again after that first day, the prince was still all anyone could talk about. If telling his stories could make the Maiden lower her weapon, what else might Alphonsus be capable of?

Each story, each speculation, each reverent compliment paid to the prince preyed on Guntram. The people had forgotten that it was he—Guntram—who'd calmed the Maiden's anger and returned Somber End's good fortunes. They'd forgotten that he'd spent ten years in the shadow of that monstrous statue. Alphonsus had been there for *barely a week*. Surrounded by the luxury he'd always dreamed of, Guntram found he still craved the fame his childhood had given him. Fame that now meant nothing.

Guntram grew bitter. He started to hate the Maiden. Wasn't it he who'd kept her company for so long? Wasn't it he who'd eased her silent temper with his stories?

So focused was he on his anger, Guntram hadn't noticed the hollow ache just behind his heart. When he'd had nothing else, he'd had the Maiden. Even as the other villagers had praised him for thwarting the Maiden, Guntram's parents had remained unimpressed. They'd mocked the boy's so-called achievements. That had hurt. And for years to come, Guntram would confuse the village's good fortunes with the Maiden's love for him. He was angry the statue had moved for the prince. But he was heartbroken to think he'd lost her love.

When Guntram realized there was nothing he could do to influence the Maiden, he turned his silent fury to the one person he *could* influence. The person who'd stolen his glory. Prince Alphonsus.

And even though it had been he himself who had set the boy on his path to acclaim, Guntram's toxic imagination festered inside. With each day, his hatred blossomed with thorns that pierced his every organ. He could feel them pressing up from within, threatening to burst through his skin. He knew he would do anything to keep from losing everything he loved.

Guntram considered volunteering to be the Maiden's guardian again. He would go to the empress and suggest that Alphonsus, as future emperor, was too important to waste on such a trivial task as talking to a statue. The prince should be in the palace, learning how to rule.

But even if the empress agreed, he knew the people would not. It was Alphonsus whose stories had made the Maiden lower her weapon. Surely they would never want to go back to Guntram, who, in ten years, had never stirred the Maiden to move. He pictured the villagers booing his arrival and demanding the return of the prince.

No. He could never return to being guardian and regain the adoration he once enjoyed as long as another— a *better*—guardian lived.

Prince Alphonsus had to die.

Oh, yes, the prince's sudden death might mean that the empress would send Guntram back to Somber End to resume his duties as guardian. But surely he could make her see that it would be best to send him to tell the Maiden stories during the day and allow him to come back to his royal apartments each night. Then he would have the best of everything he loved.

Everything he believed he deserved.

At the end of the prince's first week as guardian, on the night of the first new moon of summer, Guntram tiptoed through the corridors to the chambers below the palace. It was here that the royal apothecary toiled each day to provide the empress with any number of unguents and ointments guaranteed to soothe an aching head or induce the deepest slumber.

Guntram pried open the lock on the apothecary's storage room. Candle in one hand, he picked through bottle after bottle of sleeping draughts and salves until he found what he was looking for: a crescent-shaped flask with a wax stopper. A small tag on the bottle read RAVENSTRIKE.

Mixed with essence of jannis root, filtered through a sheep's stomach, and diluted with liver oil, ravenstrike was a potent remedy for fever. Unfiltered, unaltered, unmixed in any way, however, ravenstrike was the deadliest poison in the land.

Absorbed through the skin, a thimbleful could render a man Guntram's size unconscious for months. And if he ever awoke, he would surely be an invalid the rest of his life. That same dose would easily kill a boy the size of the prince.

Shrouding himself in a hooded cloak, Guntram scaled the palace gates and made his way to Somber End. Darkness blanketed the sleepy village. The Margrave scampered nimbly among the shadows, fearful of any eyes that might be prying at this late hour.

At the village center, he slithered across the roundel to the base of the Onyx Maiden. This was the first time he'd seen the "miracle" for himself. She really had lowered her weapon. It only made Guntram angrier.

With a knife, he dug out the wax stopper and turned the ravenstrike bottle upside down. The thick poison twinkled in the dim light as it poured out, completely covering the statue's base.

Guntram slunk out of Somber End and moved along the path toward the silhouette of the palace in the distance. Atop the palace's tallest tower, two lanterns—one blue, one green—shone out through a window in the turret. He'd never noticed that before. A signal of some sort?

That night, Guntram's sleep teemed with dark visions. Not with thoughts of ravenstrike or his callous deed. No. He couldn't shake the image of those two lights from the tower high above. So bright and unflinching. As if the castle had eyes.

As if the castle had seen what he'd done.

7

The Second Miracle

THERE WASN'T A SHOE TO BE SEEN AMONG THE CHILDREN OF Somber End.

Even though a week had passed since the Maiden had first lowered her terrible flail and there had been no further signs of her movement, the people of Somber End couldn't stop singing the prince's praises. In honor of Alphonsus, every girl and boy had begun walking barefoot wherever they went.

Whenever the people could see him, Alphonsus smiled broadly. He assured them that no harm would befall Somber End as long as there was breath in his body.

It was all an act. Alphonsus was more afraid now than he'd ever been before.

Each night, he stood in front of his mirror and watched the clock in his chest run backward. He worried it was stealing his very life, snatching away minutes and hours with each innocent *brrda-tick-click*.

That first night, he'd run through the palace to find his mother. He had to show her what was happening. He had to hear her say that everything would be okay.

But he stopped just short of knocking on her door. In the time it had taken to discover the backward-running clock and sprint to his mother's bedchambers, a thousand possible explanations for the clock's strange movement had sliced through his mind like knives. One repeated over and over: *It means I'm dying.*

He couldn't tell his mother this. With rumors of something dark stirring in the Hinterlands, his mother had the safety of her people already weighing heavily on her thoughts. And he had seen how Dagmar's death had hurt the empress. He didn't want to worry her over something she clearly couldn't fix. He had to keep yet another secret until a solution presented itself.

So he kept going to the village. He kept talking to the Maiden. He kept pretending nothing had changed, even though everything had changed.

Every night, after returning from Somber End,

he went to the tower to hang the lanterns. It was more important than ever that Birgit complete her mission. He wished now that he'd asked her to send letters, updating him of her progress. But he hadn't heard a word since she left. He was starting to wonder if the clockmaker could ever be found.

He was starting to wonder if Birgit was dead.

The day after the first new moon of summer, Alphonsus went to the village as he'd done every morning that week. The usual crowd had gathered to watch. The burgermeister's deputies had hung waist-high banners around the edge of the roundel to make sure no one got too close to the prince. When the boy approached the statue, a roar went up from the crowd, and they immediately fell silent again as Alphonsus sat cross-legged before the Maiden.

The base of the statue glistened, moist and slick with what the prince assumed was morning dew. Alphonsus paid it no mind. He started whispering to the Maiden. He knew the spectators were leaning over the banner, straining to hear. But he'd always kept his words private. He didn't want anyone knowing what was said.

"It's still running backward," Alphonsus told the Maiden. "I'd really hoped it would have fixed itself by now. This happened when we touched. Did you have anything to do with it?"

He'd asked this every day since the first. He didn't expect an answer, but he kept asking because he wanted one. Even if getting it was improbable.

It occurred to Alphonsus that he'd never told the Maiden about Birgit. Not even his mother knew the story of how he'd sent the huntress on a mission.

"I miss Birgit," he said softly. "I'm worried that my clock running backward means I'm running out of time. I think it means I'm dying. I need her to come back with the clockmaker who can save me. Guntram Steinherz says you can make things happen. If you can't fix my clock, can you help Birgit find the clockmaker?"

But even this, his second deep secret, didn't prompt the Maiden to act. Alphonsus grew sullen. He knew he didn't have time to waste waiting for the Maiden. In all likelihood, she couldn't do anything. He was on his own.

At the end of the day, shoulders slumped down under the weight of the world, Alphonsus rose. "I'll be back tomorrow," he droned. He reached out to touch the statue's base.

The sound of stone grinding on stone rent the air. In the space between the prince's heartbeats, the Maiden had pivoted at the waist, reached out, and closed her open hand around his arm. She held it still, the boy's outstretched fingers just an inch from the base.

This time, everyone had *seen* the statue move. Screams

rang out. The day they feared had come. They were about to receive the terrible reckoning that had been promised.

Terror kept Alphonsus glued to the spot. The Maiden's viselike grip didn't hurt, but the cold onyx bit into his flesh. He stared up. The statue's face hadn't changed. She looked just as malevolent as ever. But for the first time, Alphonsus saw something else in those harsh eyes. It was a look he'd seen on his mother's face. The one she reserved for when she was being fiercely protective.

Silence fell as everyone realized that the Maiden had stopped moving again. She held the prince firmly but made no move to lay waste to Somber End.

Alphonsus held his breath. As he squirmed to try to free himself from the Maiden's closed fist, a dove flew down and landed on the statue's base. A second later, it squawked and dropped dead onto the ground below.

The prince peered at the substance on the base. It was thick and unmoving. He'd dismissed it as dew. But the base had remained wet all day long. He looked down at the dead dove and made the only logical connection: It was poison. Someone who knew he touched the base of the statue at the end of every day had tried to poison him.

She saved me, Alphonsus realized.

Suddenly, the ground rumbled and shook. People ran indoors. Chunks of stone broke off from the Maiden, falling and shattering as they hit the roundel below.

Alphonsus tugged and tugged to free himself from the Maiden's grip, desperate to be clear of the falling rocks, but she held him fast. The prince fell to his knees and covered his head with his only available arm.

It took Alphonsus several moments to realize the earthquake had stopped. Slowly, doors to houses opened and the people of Somber End stuck their noses out. The two royal guards who accompanied the prince each day ran to the roundel to tend to their liege.

But they froze before the statue, gaping up at it in wonder. Soon, others approached, drawn in by curiosity, and they, too, stopped in place and stared. Alphonsus peeked out, pulling his arm from over his head. When he saw all eyes fixed on the Maiden, he looked up.

The Onyx Maiden remained mostly intact. The bits of stone that had broken away had come from her chest, exposing a small, round opening.

Inside that opening: a clock.

And it ran backward.

8

In the Shadow of the Hexen Woods

THE FEW MEMORIES OF HER FATHER THAT ESME STILL possessed were hazy at best. The pictures she could summon in her mind had soft edges, as if seen through bleary morning eyes. The sounds seemed distant and limited to hushed whispers. Still, she clung to these scraps of memory like an infant to its favorite blanket. They brought her comfort.

If she concentrated, she could vaguely recall her father—a man named Klaus, with soft, watery eyes—clutching her closely to his hip as the caravan of wizards fled Rheinvelt all those years ago, making their way across the moonlit countryside.

Or maybe she'd been told the story so many times by the Hierophant Collective, she just imagined that she could remember. Over the years, she feared her recollections had been tainted by fictions, her own and those of others who'd known Klaus. She feared those memories now replayed more of what she *wanted* her father to be and less of who he actually was.

For example, the dreams of her father seemed more like a fairy tale than anything real. She could see her father laughing and waving his arms, glowing magical sigils dancing in the air over his head.

That, of course, was impossible. Klaus had died before he could teach Esme magic. Everything Esme had learned had been under the guidance of the Hierophant Collective, the wise council who ruled all Hierophants. But still, as strange as the dreams seemed, they also felt true.

Esme had no memories of her mother. She'd never even met the woman.

That was about to change—in the most horrible way possible.

Esme stood on the edge of the dirt road she'd been following since leaving Schneegart, her toes touching the border of the Hexen Woods. She stared long and hard into the forest. It looked like any other grove. She'd expected it to be filled with gnarled black trees and impenetrable darkness. But, if anything, it seemed light and inviting. Which only gave her pause.

She knew she had to enter. Still, she lingered, studying the shaded copse. "The moment you set foot in the Hexen Woods," the Hierophant Collective had said, just before Esme started her journey, "the protections we have bestowed upon you will be lifted."

The Collective consisted of five Hierophants, forever shrouded in white hoods and black veils that covered their faces. Men? Women? A combination of both? No one knew anymore. When the Collective spoke, they did so as one, a single mass voice that rattled like locust chatter.

"But isn't that when I'll need them the most?" Esme had asked.

"The Balance of these charms forces you to tell the truth," the Collective had said. "When you face the Nachtfrau, you will be glad for the ability to lie."

The stories of her mother's powers were legend. Without the ability to lie, Esme didn't see having much chance against a woman who, it was said, could invoke a sigil's power without speaking its cant. She would have to lie to get her mother to trust her. And that meant going into the Hexen Woods with only the protections her own mastery of magic afforded.

"Have faith in your abilities," the Collective had said, their parting words.

Faith in her ability to wield magic had never been a problem for Esme. Gaining someone's trust and then killing them . . . she had far less faith in her ability to do that. But it had to be done. The fate of all the Hierophants rested on her shoulders alone.

With this knowledge pulsing in her brain, Esme stepped into the Hexen Woods.

She immediately felt something grip her ankle, hard and unyielding. Her leg was yanked skyward, lifting her into the air with her head dangling. It felt like she'd stepped into a snare, but she could see no rope. Her limp body flew higher and higher until she emerged above the tree line, where she froze.

A glowing mist—black and green—swirled around her. As it did, bright globes of white light shot from her body. The departure of each left Esme feeling nauseated and vulnerable. One by one, the Collective's protections were being stripped away. Her invisible guardians dispersed and dissipated. And when the glowing mists had finished their job, she fell.

Tree branches scratched her arms and face during her free fall. But Esme stayed focused. Her fingers danced, tracing sigils in the air as she shouted their cants. The mossy earth below grew nearer.

Suddenly, the ground split open and a gust of wind rose up to cushion her fall, mere feet from impact. Esme gasped at the abrupt stop, then sighed with relief as the geyser of air she'd summoned gently lowered her to the ground. Shaken, the young Hierophant crawled to a nearby tree and slumped with her back against it.

She fumbled for the flask at her belt. In half a minute, she'd downed its entire supply of water. This was the Balance for manipulating earth and air; she was dehydrated.

Getting her senses back, Esme stood. There were no pathways through the woods. She'd have to make her own. Selecting a lengthy fallen tree branch, Esme fashioned herself a walking stick and started the trek through the forest.

She rehearsed what she would say to the Nachtfrau when they came face-to-face. It was imperative she sound sincere. She had to do everything possible to gain the sorceress's trust. And then, when she'd earned it, when the old woman's defenses were down . . .

"Your mother can see you coming, you know."

Esme whirled around. There, on the rock she'd just passed, lay a fox. She swore it hadn't been there a moment ago. But now it was, covered in golden-caramel fur, paws stretched out and crossed. It looked bored.

"You seem surprised, cub," the fox said. "This is your mother's domain. Everything here—the leaves you brush up against, the sand you tread on—is part of her. There is nothing in these woods that wouldn't betray you at her word. You should consider that."

Esme pressed her thumb and little finger together and spread the other three fingers wide. The fox scoffed.

"Going to favor us with a spot of magic?" it asked. "Go on, then. From the hand position, I'm guessing maybe a schwarzdrachen spell. Curl your thumb a bit more—there's a lass. You don't want to accidentally cast a regnen spell by mistake. The sigils and cants are so alike, don't you think? But, really, you shouldn't waste your time."

Esme paused, then lowered her hand. "I can cast it," she said confidently. The schwarzdrachen spell was the most complex magic she knew. It involved each finger moving independently to trace five different sigils at once. She had to cant each sigil's name perfectly and in rhythm to get it all just right. The question was: Could she do it before the fox struck?

The fox sniffed. "Of course you can cast it. No doubt the Hierophant Collective were very thorough in their training. You can cast that spell with little thought, I'd imagine. What I want to know is: Do you understand the Balance?"

"I'm not here to waste time talking to foxes," the girl said, ignoring the animal's question. She wasn't about to betray how astounded she was. Enchanting animals to talk? Clearly, the stories she'd heard about her mother's abilities were gravely understated. She hadn't even known that sort of magic existed.

Esme turned her back to the fox and continued ahead through the woods. She hadn't gotten far when the fox poked its pointed nose out from behind a tree just ahead.

"She's been expecting you, cub. For quite some time now. She's always known it would come to this. But, I must say, you're looking rather piqued. Not up to snuff? Are you sure you're prepared for what you've come to do?"

"And what would you know about it, you craven beast?" Esme roared. She spun on her heel, pulling out her dagger. If she couldn't scare the pest away, she'd have its guts for garters.

But the fox was already gone. A tall woman wearing a cloak of colorful woven leaves stood where the animal had just been. The woman, with a long, thin face, paused to brush bits of golden-caramel fur from her shoulder. Then she cast her gaze on Esme and said, "'Craven beast'? Is that any way to speak to your mother?"

9

Blood Ties

"SO, YOU'RE MY ASSASSIN."

Esme gasped, suddenly very aware how cool the steel hilt of the dagger in her hand felt. The blade seemed heavier than usual. Perhaps that was to be expected when face-to-face with the woman you were sent to kill.

Or maybe that was only when that woman was also your mother.

The sorceress squinted, looked the girl up and down, and sniffed. "You've got my chin. Sorry about that, by the way. But the rest of you? That's all your father." Her voice smiled. She sounded very much like she missed Esme's father.

As the Collective had predicted, Esme was sincerely grateful for the ability to lie once more. "No one sent me. No one even knows I'm gone. I came because you're my mother. I need to know where I came from."

She'd rehearsed every aspect of her story—the look of shock at the suggestion that she was capable of murder, the earnest eyes pleading for a mother's love.

The Nachtfrau bared her teeth. In a blur, she thrust her hand up over her head, her fingers forming a claw. Before Esme could even summon a protective sigil, the light in the forest disappeared. It didn't just become night; all light had vanished, leaving the young Hierophant in complete blackness.

One by one, pairs of glowing eyes appeared in the darkness. Esme could sense movement all around, could hear snarls and growls and hisses. Something brushed against her leg.

"Do not lie to me, girl!"

The Nachtfrau's voice, now terrible and booming, came from everywhere: over Esme's shoulder, directly ahead, from beneath her feet.

Esme clenched her fists. Her fingers itched to trace an illumination symbol and cast off the darkness. But if her plan was to work, she couldn't let on how adept she'd become at magic. It was important the Nachtfrau not see her as any sort of threat.

"Okay," she whispered meekly into the blackness. "I'm sorry. I'll tell you the truth."

As quickly as it had shrouded the forest, the darkness bled away. Esme could once again see her mother. Only now, instead of standing before the girl, the Nachtfrau sat on a throne made of tree roots, vines, and rocks that had seemingly risen up out of the ground. The sorceress studied her daughter.

"I can only imagine what they've told you about me."

"They said—"

The Nachtfrau raised a hand. "Please, if you don't mind, I'd *rather* imagine what they told you."

Esme bowed her head. "You're right. They sent me to kill you."

"Sending a child to kill her own mother. Yes, that sounds like the Collective."

Anger flashed in the girl's eyes. "You didn't give them much choice. Did you?" She immediately regretted the outburst. Admitting the nature of her mission was meant to gain the Nachtfrau's trust. Getting upset could only undo that.

The Nachtfrau's lips twisted into a smile. "Yes. I understand they're having some troubles in their new home. Trapped in a valley filled with eternal winter. Fixed to the spot. As if by magic."

"You cursed us." Esme tried to sound matter-of-fact. But her deep resentment was hard to hide. "Almost ten years ago, you cast a spell that prevents any Hierophant from leaving the valley. To do so means death."

"But *you're* here. *You* left the North Lands."

"We both know why I was able to leave."

"Yes, I'm sure you think you do. I'm sure the Collective taught you many things. Let's see how much, shall we? What is the first law of magic?"

"Magic cannot bring life." The words came out involuntarily. It was any Hierophant's automatic response to this question, which was at the very core of their training. The laws of magic had been the first things drilled into Esme as soon as she could speak.

"The second law?"

"Magic cannot reverse death."

The Nachtfrau's tongue rolled around the inside of her cheeks. She almost looked impressed.

"Why does that surprise you?" Esme asked, insulted to think her mother believed her incapable of mastering this very simple knowledge.

"That you understand it doesn't surprise me," the Nachtfrau replied. "That the Collective bothered to teach it to you does. They don't always have a taste for their own laws."

She'll tell you lies, the Collective had warned Esme. *She'll say anything to twist your mind to her will. You must be strong.* Esme kept her face plain. She couldn't let the sorceress see her angry again.

The Nachtfrau grunted. "So the Collective sent you to end the spell that's kept them trapped for almost ten years now. And there are only two ways any spell can end. It can be voluntarily lifted by the person who cast it. Or it ends when the caster dies."

"Only if the caster is killed by a blood relative," Esme said softly. "Any other kind of death, and the curse goes on forever."

The blood ties in the magic practiced by the Hierophants ran deep. It was the blood she shared with her mother that had made it possible for Esme to leave the cursed valley unscathed. That same blood made her the only person who could end the curse.

The sorceress peered into her daughter's eyes, never blinking or looking away. After several moments, she sniffed and said, "Well then, you'd best get on with it. Would you prefer I stand or sit?"

"I . . . I . . ."

"Eyes open? Eyes shut? Your call, really. This is more about your convenience than my comfort."

Esme blinked back her confusion. The sorceress

was taunting her. She remembered her dagger, still in hand, and gripped it tightly. The Nachtfrau rolled her eyes.

"You were getting ready to cast a schwarzdrachen spell just moments ago. Surely you're not going to kill me with something so"—she glared at the dagger—"*common*."

Esme paused. She doubted the Nachtfrau was really just going to sit there and let her attack. The sorceress was up to something. Until she figured out what, Esme had to be cautious.

"I'm sorry it's come to this," she said, holding the dagger out threateningly.

"Of course," the Nachtfrau said, "you could just *ask* me to end the spell."

The dagger nearly dropped from the young Hierophant's hand. She didn't like any of this. How calm the Nachtfrau was. How agreeable.

"Oh, you'd just do that, would you?" Esme asked.

"You'd be surprised what a parent will do for their child." Had Esme not been so focused on her own anger, she might have noticed a wistful lilt to the Nachtfrau's tone.

Esme chose to call the sorceress's bluff. She slid her dagger back into its sheath. "Fine, then. Release the spell on the Hierophants."

The Nachtfrau tsked. "You thought it would be that easy? What about the Balance?"

"The Balance doesn't apply if you release a spell."

"Oh, but it does. *All* magic is give-and-take. I take away the spell, you give me something. Sorry, but that's how it's going to be. Even for my daughter. I need you to get me something."

Esme balked. "You're the most powerful Hierophant in generations. You can have anything you want. Why must *I* get it?"

"Alas, I cannot leave the Hexen Woods. I have used all the magic I know to fortify this land and keep me protected. The Balance is, I can never leave. I am tied to these woods. If I leave, I die."

"What do you want?"

The Nachtfrau waved a hand. Soundlessly, a small patch of earth at Esme's feet disgorged a lump of rock. It floated up until it hung eye level to the girl. Bit by bit, small chunks of stone dropped away, as if a veiled sculptor was busy carving her latest masterpiece. Moments later, a miniature statue of a woman in armor, carrying a flail, spun slowly before Esme.

"At the southern edge of the Hexen Woods lies the town of Somber End. A maiden made of onyx towers over the center of the village. I want you to bring me the heart of the Onyx Maiden."

Esme eyed the small figurine. "A statue has a heart?"

"Goodness, girl, use your imagination. Chisel through to the statue's center and bring me what you find there. Do I have to explain everything to you? Surely this should be simple for someone taught personally by the Collective."

Esme looked up sharply. How could her mother possibly know about her training? And how much did she know about Esme's abilities?

The Nachtfrau snapped her fingers. The miniature statue crumbled to gray dust, which fell and covered the toes of the girl's boots. "Now . . . do we have a deal?"

Esme didn't believe for a second that her mother would willingly end the spell on the Hierophants. Why else did she cast it in the first place if she was so quick to agree to end it? But going on this little quest would give Esme a chance to earn her mother's trust. She would prove that she meant the sorceress no harm. And then, when her mother believed in her, Esme would do what she was sent to do.

"If I get you this," Esme said, "you'll end the spell?"

The Nachtfrau closed her eyes solemnly. "Do this, and we can put this whole affair to rest."

Deep down, a tiny part of Esme hoped her mother would honor the bargain. Even given everything the Nachtfrau had done to the Hierophants, Esme was reluctant to kill. But she knew, if it came down to it, she would have no choice.

"I'll do it."

The sorceress clapped her hands together. "Excellent! You should leave at once. Head due south." At a gesture from the sorceress, the nearby flora—bushes, saplings, and tall grass—moved aside, creating a clear path for Esme to follow. "You won't miss Somber End. Should be there by sundown. Oh, and you'll need this." From within her robes, the Nachtfrau produced a small cube, just slightly larger than both of Esme's fists mashed together. Each side had been crafted from a different piece of gray-white bone and bound together with crystallized tree sap.

Esme regarded the box. "What is it?"

"You'll need something to put the heart in," the Nachtfrau said. "This will do nicely."

When Esme took the box, a soft tingle met her touch. Each side of the cube bore intricately carved whorls that twisted in on each other. The lid connected with a single long copper hinge along the top. It was at once beautiful and grotesque to look at. Most notable, the box seemed familiar somehow. It clearly thrummed with magic, which made her suspicious.

"This is enchanted," she announced. "What does it do?"

But when she looked up, the Nachtfrau was gone, an eddy of leaves swirling where the sorceress had once stood.

It could be a trap, Esme thought. Perhaps the box was rigged to explode when she opened it in Somber End. If that was the case, she needed to open it now. If the Nachtfrau was tied to the forest as she claimed, an explosion here would certainly harm the sorceress.

Esme traced three sigils in the air over her head and whispered their cants. Ghostly echoes of the sigils shimmered, then showered down on her. This *should* protect her. She hoped. Steeling her jaw, she flipped open the box's lid.

A gust of air—musty and rank—belched forth from within, as if the box had been holding a breath. Esme gagged as the acrid smell forced its way into her lungs. The box was empty. Her shoulders slumped in relief. She was just about to close it again when a voice—as soft as it was sonorous—rose up from within.

> *"When nights pass as hours the same*
> *The end of time will start*
> *A sacrifice is all that saves*
> *The counterclockwise heart"*

Esme felt as though something had reached through her chest. The box shook in her grasp. The rhyme meant nothing to her. In fact, after the first few words, she'd stopped listening to what was being said. All she could hear was the voice.

It was her father's.

10

The Maiden's Betrayal

THE THRONE ROOM ECHOED WITH TALK OF WAR.

The empress's most trusted counselors had gathered to discuss it. Angry voices fought to be heard over the din. The minister of intelligence repeated what her spies had heard: the creatures in the Hinterlands were massing near the borders near Somber End, a sure sign they intended to invade. Rheinvelt had to strike first. The minister of war insisted just as loudly that Rheinvelt was ready for invasion but that they should not be the first to lash out. Everyone with an opinion—and that was every minister, every advisor, and every viceroy and grand duchess—shouted it at top volume.

All except the Margrave. Guntram Steinherz sat silently, hearing none of the debate. Through the tumult, his eyes never left the throne room door. Any moment now, that door would fly open and someone would enter to announce that the prince was dead. Slain by merely touching the Maiden.

There would be hue and cry. Lives in villages and cities throughout Rheinvelt would halt, the people of the empire consumed with grief. Fear would grip the villagers of Somber End. They would demand Guntram's immediate return to protect them. He would graciously go to them each morning, talk to the statue all day, and return each night to the indulgences of the palace.

Best of all: If anyone discovered the ravenstrike, the Hinterland beasts would be blamed for the prince's assassination. Guntram would never be suspected.

Finally, after an hour of listening to her advisors' caterwauling, Empress Sabine massaged her temples and shouted, "Enough! You are dismissed. We will reconvene tomorrow at this time. I expect to hear less shouting and more reason."

One by one, Sabine's advisors bowed and exited. When Guntram turned to leave, the empress beckoned.

"You were very quiet, Margrave," she said. "I brought you to the palace to share your wisdom. Why so stingy?"

"Forgive me, Majesty," Guntram said, forcing a smile, "but with all the noise, how can you be sure my voice wasn't drowning in the clamor?"

The empress arched an eyebrow. "Well, it's just the two of us now. Tell me what you think we should do."

Guntram swallowed hard. He wished he'd been paying more attention during the discussion. When he'd first been asked to become the queen's advisor, his thoughts had focused solely on the luxuries that would be afforded him by moving into the royal palace. He hadn't really considered what advice he could possibly give. He knew nothing of wars or diplomacy or the Hinterlands. In fact, it had only just occurred to him that he knew very little of the world beyond Somber End.

"I'm afraid," he said slowly, "that the debate has left my thoughts scattered. Perhaps, Majesty, if I could have solitude to think things through more carefully . . ."

He searched Sabine's face for suspicion. He feared that any moment now she'd realize her folly in inviting a commoner to serve on her council.

Instead, she nodded. "You and I could both use time to clear our heads. Tomorrow, then. I look forward to hearing your thoughts, Margrave."

Guntram exhaled loudly once the empress had departed, leaving him alone in the throne room. He'd bought a little time. It was all he'd need. Any moment now, word of the prince's death would distract the empress from wanting to hear his thoughts on—

"Mother!"

Guntram turned as Alphonsus burst through the door and ran across the throne room, his bare feet slapping on the stone floor. Just behind him, the two guards that accompanied him each day to Somber End stumbled in, their faces twisted in confusion. Guntram's stomach clenched in shock and anger. How had the ravenstrike failed?

"Mother!" Alphonsus bellowed, stopping just short of the throne. "Margrave, where is the empress?"

Guntram stiffened, as if a cold steel rod had been driven down his spine. His eyes bored into the prince. "The empress isn't here, Your Highness."

The boy grabbed Guntram's arm. "She moved again, Margrave. The Maiden moved. *She saved me.*"

Alphonsus explained how he'd reached out for the base but the Maiden had stopped him from touching some poison, which killed a bird moments later. He spoke quickly and animatedly, ending with, "And when the onyx fell away, there was a clock in her chest!"

The moment he said this, the prince immediately pulled his lips tight, as if he'd said more than he'd intended. If Guntram had been paying attention to this, he might have questioned why the boy seemed so excited to find a clock in the statue's chest. Or why Alphonsus might quickly regret sharing this news. But those questions were far from Guntram's mind.

Every drop of blood in the Margrave's body had turned to pure rage. The Maiden had moved for the welp *again*. She'd saved him from the ravenstrike. At this point, it was impossible for him to imagine anything other than the Maiden doing this to spite him.

Guntram pictured the people of Somber End laughing at him. *She never moved for* you, he could hear them say. *If your life had been in danger, she wouldn't have moved to save* you. He'd become a joke.

None of this had happened, of course. The slights existed solely in the Margrave's fertile imagination. But the stories he'd told the statue as a child—his dreams of glory—had all come true. Why should he believe the villagers' taunts wouldn't also come to pass?

Fighting to contain his anger, Guntram looked to the guards for confirmation.

"I saw it myself, Margrave," said the first guard, a round-faced man named Tomas. "Everyone in town could see it. A large clock, running backward."

"The people are saying it's another miracle," the second guard—named Uwe—added. "They think the prince is their savior."

Miracle. Savior. The words conjured fire and hatred at the base of Guntram's skull.

"I need to show my mother," the prince said. "She needs to see the clock."

Guntram bit into his lower lip until he could taste blood. The last thing he needed was for the empress to see for herself how beloved the prince had become. *He* should be the one being lauded. *He* should be the miraculous savior.

Now, Guntram could have gone to the Maiden. He could have told her how hurt he was that she'd never done for him what she'd done for the prince. He could have let loose with his feelings to the statue and hope he'd come to understand why she was doing this. But Guntram continued to confuse his sadness for anger. The love he'd imagined—the one thing that had sustained him for so long—was gone.

At that moment, Guntram had never wanted anything more than to see the Maiden destroyed completely. Knowing that impossible, he decided to do the next best thing: hurt her. She had taken away something that was rightfully his. Now he would take something she was claiming as her own.

"Fetch the empress," Guntram said to the guards. Then he leaned in so only they could hear him. "I'm worried about the boy. I fear the Maiden has bewitched him somehow. He seems . . . obsessed with the statue. Get the empress quickly before something terrible happens to him. She's in the garden."

The guards ran from the throne room. Guntram shut the doors behind them. When they got to the gardens and couldn't find the empress, it would take them a while to locate her. It was all the time the Margrave needed.

Guntram slowly advanced on the prince, smiling. "A clock, you say? In her chest?"

Alphonsus nodded. He rummaged through a satchel at his waist and pulled out a chunk of onyx nearly the size of his own head. "The ground shook, and pieces of the Maiden fell away."

The Margrave took the rock in his hand. It would be so easy to smash the prince's skull with one swift move. But no. If he was to convince the empress that the prince had died because of the Maiden's magic, he could leave no marks.

"I'm going back to Somber End," Alphonsus announced. "Send my mother there at once—"

"I don't think that would be wise, Your Highness," Guntram said, moving to block the prince's departure. "This sounds very dangerous to me. A clock? Running backward? An ominous portent, surely."

Alphonsus scowled at the Margrave. "The clock doesn't mean the Maiden is going to harm anyone."

"Your Highness, we've known for years that the Maiden is a threat to the empire. I think the clock proves it."

Alphonsus snatched the onyx back and placed it in his satchel. "No, it doesn't. Clocks aren't dangerous."

Guntram took a step forward, hands outstretched while the boy's attention was on the satchel. "And how can you be so sure? You've been with the Maiden a week. I've known her for ten years, and I'm telling you that clock means—"

The boy looked up with a viciousness none had ever seen on the prince. It was enough to startle Guntram.

Alphonsus dropped his satchel, removed his shirt, and threw it to the floor. "The Maiden is no threat because *I* am no threat," the prince said firmly.

There, in the center of the boy's chest, Guntram saw a clock. A backward-running clock. The Maiden, it seemed, hadn't just saved the boy. She had *marked* him. She had imbued him with her power, the power Guntram had spent his life longing for.

All for this boy. This brat. Ten years of Guntram's life had meant nothing to the Maiden. Ten years giving up his childhood. Ten years languishing in poverty created by the Maiden's presence. Ten years of ridicule from his parents. Along comes the prince, and those ten years vanished as if they'd never happened. A life wasted.

The Maiden had given Guntram his every wish but she'd *chosen* Alphonsus to receive her power. She had betrayed Guntram.

Blind with rage, the Margrave wrapped his hands around the boy's throat and squeezed. As the boy gasped for air, Guntram imagined what he'd say to the empress. *He kept talking about the Maiden until he collapsed. I tried to save him . . .*

But then, Alphonsus thrust his arms up between Guntram's wrists in a blow strong enough to break the Margrave's hold. Pivoting, the boy spun and kicked, driving his foot into Guntram's stomach. The man doubled over and grunted. He had forgotten that Birgit Freund had taught the boy to fight.

Alphonsus tried to run, but Guntram put himself between the prince and the door. "It should have been me," Guntram growled as he bore down on the prince.

The boy ducked as Guntram swung at him. Any bravado he'd gained from breaking Guntram's hold bled from his face. Alphonsus was terrified. *Good*, Guntram thought.

"Her power should be mine," the Margrave said as the prince ran behind the throne. "You don't deserve—"

As he rounded the throne, Guntram found nothing. The prince had vanished. Guntram poked at the walls and the floor. He remembered the lords and ladies telling him the palace was filled with secret passages known only to the royals. Surely, the prince had used one to escape.

He had to find the boy.

Just outside, two sets of armored boots echoed in the corridor, approaching quickly. The prince's personal guard was returning.

Acting swiftly, Guntram overturned the prince's discarded satchel, selected a large piece of onyx, and struck his own temple. Warm blood gushed down his cheek. He threw himself to the floor as the guards entered the room.

"The prince," Guntram cried out weakly. "He's gone mad! He attacked me. He's been possessed by the Maiden."

"Where is he?" Uwe asked.

There was only one place the boy would go now.

"Come with me to Somber End. We have to stop him before he wakens the Maiden!"

11

The Prince's Flight

Brrda-tick-click! Brrda-tick-click!

Alphonsus crawled on all fours, scrambling blindly down a black passage made of earth and rock. He couldn't see a thing. Moist soil squished under his fingernails every time he clawed at the ground, pulling himself forward. He struggled to breathe in the hot, musty underground air.

Brrda-tick-click! Brrda-tick-click!

The damp earth seemed to absorb all sound, save his ragged breathing. The silence turned the soft ticking in his chest into a cannon's report. He hated the clock more than ever now. Alphonsus knew that when anyone else was terrified, their heart raced and hammered within.

But not him. There was only the maddening even tempo that seemed calm despite the prince knowing he was far from calm.

Brrda-tick-click! Brrda-tick-click!

Every so often, something long and thin and slimy brushed his cheeks from above. *It's a root*, he told himself. *A root dangling down from the ceiling of the tunnel.* At least, that's what he hoped it was.

They're teeth, something in the back of his brain whispered. *The tunnel is going to eat you before you make it out. Don't you know the earth eats cowards?*

He blocked out the voice and tried to focus on what he knew. Like how the tunnel would lead him to safety. Like how he'd find the assistance he needed in Somber End.

The prince charged forward, knowing Guntram could overpower him if he went back. He cast occasional glances over his shoulder into the blackness behind him, half afraid he'd find the Margrave close behind. But no. That wasn't possible.

Just before Dagmar had left on her trip to the Outer Valleys—a journey that would prove to be her last—she took Alphonsus on a tour of their palace. She showed her son the most secure areas to go in case of an attack. She showed the boy every room where the imperatrix had hidden weapons for emergencies. And she showed Alphonsus a secret passage behind the throne.

"Only the empress and I know about this," Dagmar had said. "Now you know too. Should you ever need to escape the palace, this passage will take you to an underground tunnel that leads to Somber End. There, you will be safe."

Alphonsus had never questioned why he might one day need to "escape" the palace. Now, everything he'd been told made sense. There was always the possibility that the imperial family might one day face danger in their own home. He'd been taught the word—*insurrection*—but he'd never dreamed he'd come to know exactly what it meant. And he certainly never thought the Margrave would turn out to be a traitor. Under his breath, he cursed the day the empress brought that man into the palace.

The prince had done as Dagmar had instructed. He'd escaped. Alphonsus knew his next move was clear: get to Somber End, rally support, and arrest Guntram.

There was only one problem. The fear that had dominated his life for years felt far, far stronger than his resolve. A small part of him wanted to curl up right here in the tunnel and hide. The fear made it seem so very inviting. He could just disappear here in the dark, avoiding the danger he'd left behind . . .

Ahead, Alphonsus could hear the faint burble of rushing water. The prince considered. Following the sound of the water meant leaving the tunnel. And safety. But it also meant doing something he considered far worse than danger: letting Guntram win. With new vigor, he charged forward, the water getting louder the farther he went. Pinpricks of light in the distance guided him toward the exit of the tunnel, where a curtain of moss and roots blocked his way. Pushing through, he emerged from behind a small waterfall and into a stream in the woods. A familiar dirt road—the path to Somber End— sat on the shore to his left. He was almost there.

His breeches soaked, his bare feet and chest caked with mud, the ragged prince pulled himself onto the road and staggered toward the village. As he entered, he drew gasps from all who spotted him.

"Help!" he called out, his voice hoarse. "Insurrection in the palace! The empress is in danger!"

Alphonsus plowed on, toward the roundel. A crowd clutching lanterns and torches gathered to follow him. A young woman ran to get the burgermeister.

When Alphonsus arrived at the roundel, he found eight members of the constabulary surrounding the Onyx Maiden, each wielding a cudgel. The burgermeister pressed his way through the throngs of people and went straight to the prince.

"What's going on here?" Alphonsus demanded, glaring at the guards near the Maiden.

"You saw for yourself that the Maiden is starting to

awaken, Your Highness," the burgermeister said. "We needed to take precautions—"

"The Maiden isn't the problem," Alphonsus snapped. "I need your constable and deputies to return with me to the palace at once."

"Everyone step away from the prince!"

Alphonsus turned quickly to see Guntram and the prince's own personal guards enter the roundel, swords drawn. The prince pointed. "It's him! He's turned against the empress."

A burst of protestations rang out from those assembled, some expressing shock, others denying the prince's accusations against their former guardian.

"It's the prince who has turned against the empire," Guntram said, advancing slowly. "He is in league with the Onyx Maiden. She's marked him as her minion. Just look at him."

Even though Alphonsus was covered in mud and filth, it was easy to make out the silver glint of the clock embedded in his chest. The villagers who'd once followed the prince eagerly now looked very unsure.

"The prince serves the Maiden!" someone from the crowd shouted.

"He's evil!"

"The Maiden has made the prince as she is!"

Soon, everyone was calling out. Even the burgermeister

backed off, leaving the prince alone and surrounded by a mob that grew angrier by the second.

Alphonsus felt his confidence melt. Everyone feared him because of the clock in his chest. Because of something they didn't understand. Just as his mother had predicted.

"No," he pleaded quietly, lifting his hands. "No, I'm not evil." He walked backward as the crowd, led by Guntram, moved in.

Brrda-tick. Brrda-tick. Brrda-tick.

Alphonsus heard the soft sound over the din of the townsfolk. But it wasn't his own clock; that much was certain. He looked up to where the Maiden stood just behind him. The second hand on her backward clock ticked away. It beat in perfect time with his own, even with his extra click. For the first time in memory, the prince felt less alone.

"Help me," he whispered.

The earth rumbled. Everyone froze. A great ripping sound filled the air as, one by one, the Maiden tore her feet from the plinth on which she'd stood for ten years and lowered herself to the ground. The Maiden's head tilted back, and an unholy sound—like the death rattle of a thousand souls—issued forth from her mouth, shattering windows on every nearby house. As one, the villagers fell to their knees in terror. Overhead, the Maiden's fearsome cry seemed to summon a legion of thick black clouds. Within seconds, the village was besieged by terrible rain, powerful winds, and fierce lightning strikes.

Undeterred, Guntram continued toward Alphonsus.

With a speed most would have thought impossible of a statue so large, the Maiden raised her flail and swung it in an arc across the roundel. The sparkling tendrils hissed in a breeze of their own creation, sundering all masonry and timber in their path. When the flail's tips struck the Margrave, Guntram flew backward as though made of mere paper. The Maiden roared again. The skies grew darker, and the winds threatened to blow the roof off every building in Somber End.

"We have to leave here," Alphonsus shouted to her above the storm. He wasn't sure what else to do. If there had been a chance of convincing Somber End that he wasn't a servant of the Maiden, it had vanished. Whether he wanted it or not, they were now allies.

And he found he *did* want it. Despite all the stories he'd been told about the terrible statue, the two were clearly linked by the clocks they bore. He knew he had to explore what that meant. But to do so, they had to be away from those who would harm them.

The Maiden lowered her one free hand to the ground. Alphonsus gingerly stepped into her rough palm and held tight as she lifted him to her shoulder. The prince gripped one of her armored spikes and, fighting to see through the downpour, cast an eye back toward the royal palace in the distance. The tallest tower stood dark.

Birgit will see, the prince thought. *She'll see, and she'll return to help. Please, Birgit. You promised.*

"Let's go."

The Maiden roared a third time, calling forth hailstones the size of fists. Everyone who had cowered in fear at her feet now rose and ran for cover. With great lumbering steps, the Maiden pushed aside hay carts, scaffolding, and buildings alike. Nothing stood in her way.

Together, they disappeared into the storm-soaked landscape.

12

The Hierophant's Ally

It's an infinitum box.

Dusk had fallen. It had taken most of her journey toward Somber End before the name came back to Esme. She'd spent the better part of the day walking the length of the Hexen Woods and thinking about the strange cube given to her by the Nachtfrau. Nuggets of memory swam to the forefront of her mind. Yes, at some point during her training, Esme had heard the Hierophant Collective discuss these mystical items.

An infinitum box held extremely powerful magic, capable of divining information beyond human ken. Whoever possessed such a box could open it and ask any question. The box would then give two answers: one, the truth, and the other, a lie as Balance. Of course, it was useless with questions for which there were only two realistic answers: yes or no, left or right, up or down. But for a Hierophant needing to narrow a field of varied possibilities and willing to gamble on which of the box's responses was truthful, it could be an incredible resource.

The knowledge the boxes held, Esme had also been told, was dangerous. So dangerous, in fact, that the Collective had decreed it forbidden to create an infinitum box. Which, of course, would explain why the outlaw Nachtfrau had done just that. But Esme recalled a feeling that had nagged at her since the Collective had first mentioned the infinitum boxes. She couldn't pinpoint why exactly, but she'd always felt that the boxes weren't so much *forbidden* to create but rather that the ability to do so lay just outside the Collective's impressive abilities.

Which, again, would explain how the Nachtfrau, regarded as the most powerful Hierophant in ages, had succeeded in making one.

She'd never been told, however, that the boxes could speak unbidden. Which was exactly what *this* box did any time the lid was lifted.

She'd opened the box several more times during her trip. She had yet to ask a question. It only ever spoke that same peculiar rhyme, delivered the exact same way each time, before falling silent again. Esme didn't care that she had no idea what it meant. She wanted to hear her father's voice. When Klaus spoke in Esme's dreams, his voice was distant and hollow. When the infinitum box spoke, it was like her father was standing right there. Clear, warm, and alive.

This must have been a trick of the Nachtfrau, to throw Esme off balance. Yes, Esme could ask the box questions to aid her mission of gaining the Onyx Maiden's heart. But she was sure that each time she asked, the box would respond in her father's own soothing voice. Only someone truly evil would use Esme's affection for her father against her. Of course that someone was her mother.

Esme stopped for the first time since she'd eaten lunch and took in her surroundings. She saw immediately that something wasn't right.

She'd focused so hard on the infinitum box during her journey that she hadn't noticed she was no longer in the Hexen Woods. The lush forest floor had given way to coarse, colorless sand pockmarked with jagged stones. Rotting, twisted trees had replaced the lush pines. A dense mist snaked its way across the harsh landscape.

She'd been told to travel due south—which she believed she had—but clearly, she'd gotten lost. She should have been to the village by now. The question was: Where had she gone wrong?

And how could she get back on track?

Now that it was growing dark, she could cast a spell that would illuminate the way to Somber End. But there was something about this place that Esme didn't like. She found herself reluctant to light a lantern that might draw attention, let alone a glowing footpath that would serve as a trail directly to her. She would have to make do with the faint daylight escaping over the horizon. But she still needed to know which way to head from here.

With little choice, Esme opened the box. Her father's voice repeated the rhyme, and when it fell silent, the girl asked, "Which way is Somber End?"

The box shuddered, and her father's voice said, "*Your destination lies due south, no more than an hour away.*" Silence, and then the box continued, "*Travel east until the last rays of sunlight vanish on the horizon, and you'll have arrived.*"

She felt sick knowing that the box had used her father's voice to lie to her. Which answer was correct? She looked around. The same sight—bleak, gray wasteland, which hemorrhaged shadows—greeted her in all directions. No hints of distant towns or forest anywhere.

She'd already gone south. East seemed the more prudent course. With the setting sun to her back, Esme placed the box into her traveling sack and trudged across the barren landscape.

The rotting trees gave way to rocks—great hulking

mounds that looked as if they'd rained down from the sky—and the rocks rose up to become a canyon. The light breeze that had followed her most of the day stilled, and a silence took hold, so powerful that Esme could hear her own soft footfalls. But when she stopped to take a drink, she found that the sound of footsteps continued.

Behind her. To the left. The right. Straight ahead. The sounds of scurrying caromed off the canyon walls all around. Hands shaking, Esme flexed her fingers, ready for anything.

An ambush! she thought, her heart leaping to her throat. The Nachtfrau had sent her into a trap. She cursed herself for not striking the sorceress down when she'd had the chance.

"Face me!" Esme called into the encroaching darkness. "I'm not afraid."

Just ahead, *something* ran out from behind an O-shaped rock, headed toward her. Without thinking, the Hierophant raised her arm. Her fingers danced in the air, and she shouted a cant. The ground beneath her attacker softened, pulling the girl's adversary down into a dense quagmire and burying it up to its waist. Whatever it was—man? beast?—thrashed about in an effort to keep its head from sinking into the muck. It struck blindly at the oozing earth that now held it in a viscous cage.

Esme squinted. The canyon obscured what was left

of the setting sun, making it impossible to determine the nature of the being she'd captured. It was shaped like a human but seemed taller than most she'd ever known. Its arms were thick and powerful but not strong enough to allow the attacker to pull itself free.

Two more howls rang out. Esme whirled around to find a pair of similar creatures running at her from the side. She acted quickly, and soon these new attackers were engulfed to their shoulders in liquid earth. Another creature sneaking up from behind met the same treatment. And another. And another. Each fell to the Hierophant's defenses. The trapped beings howled mournfully, treading to keep from drowning.

One by one, more shadows emerged from hiding. Esme quickly lost count. She turned slowly in place and confirmed the worst: they had her surrounded.

As the unknown assailants grew closer, the girl watched her options run out. If she continued to pull the creatures into the earth, she risked turning the entire canyon floor into mush and trapping herself as well. The fact that several of their comrades were now trapped had done nothing to deter the advance of others. Esme had no choice. She had to start killing.

If I kill just one, she reasoned, *the others might leave.* Her eyes narrowed on the closest foe, hoping the intent in her look would be sufficient to give them pause. Setting her jaw, Esme crossed her wrists, palms out, and curled her forefingers. Two sigils, and she could end this. Their cants burned on the tip of her tongue. *Do it*, she silently urged herself. But her fingers wouldn't move. The cants lay still in her mouth.

One of the assailants howled and charged. Esme moved to summon a geyser of air that would thrust her up and out of reach. But before she could trace the sigil, something brushed past her ear from above and behind. A moment later, a long silver arrow protruded from the assailant's chest. The creature gurgled in anguish and fell to the ground, dead.

Three more arrows sliced through the air. Two disappeared into the darkness while the third buried itself in another attacker's shoulder. The remaining figures paused, then turned and ran. Esme muttered a counterspell, and the gelatinous quagmire became fine sand. The trapped creatures clawed their way out and joined the others in retreat.

Esme dropped to her knees, seized by the effects of the Balance. Sweat poured down her forehead and into her eyes, the salty brine blinding her. Sapped of her energy, she shivered until her teeth chattered. If the attackers came back now, she could offer no response.

Steadying herself on all fours, she looked to the top of the canyon wall. An early moonrise silhouetted a lone figure on the ridge above. This one looked much more human than the creatures. Esme could make out a cape and a hood, and a quiver and bow over one shoulder. The Hierophant's rescuer regarded her a moment, then scaled down the canyon wall with the prowess of a spider.

"Your skills with magic are as impressive as your mother told me," the stranger—a woman, by the voice— said as she leapt to the ground. The hood still hid her face. She tilted her head to survey the sandpits that had once held the girl's attackers. "Your skills as an assassin are perhaps best not spoken of."

"Who are you?" Esme rasped.

The woman moved to Esme quickly and knelt. She pressed the back of her hand to the girl's forehead and frowned.

"You're burning up," the woman said. She moistened a strip of cloth with water from the leather canteen on her hip and placed it on Esme's forehead.

Esme wanted to push her away, but the woman's arms were the only thing keeping the Hierophant from collapsing to the ground. "I'm fine . . . The Balance . . ." Too many spells too fast. Her blood was practically boiling. She had known this might happen. It had worried her the most about her mission from the Collective. There was a reason the advanced magic she'd learned was only taught to Hierophants who'd come of age. Sometimes, the toll collected by the Balance was more than someone so young could bear.

The fever will pass, she silently said over and over to herself. The pounding in her temples begged to differ.

"What are you doing here?" she managed to ask.

"Your mother sent me to make sure you made it safely to Somber End. I've been trailing behind since you left her. I won't hurt you. I'm here to help."

"I don't need your help."

"I disagree. You've wandered out of the Hexen Woods—out of Rheinvelt even. You crossed the border into the Hinterlands an hour ago. Of course, if you hadn't been so reluctant to kill the beasts—"

"Why didn't you say something if you knew I was off course?"

"I was ordered only to intervene if you were in danger. Once you entered the Hinterlands, I knew it wouldn't be long."

Esme sat up on her knees. "If you'd spoken up, I wouldn't have been in danger."

The woman's face was still hidden, but the Hierophant could hear a smile in her voice. "Then I never would have had the pleasure of your *charming* company."

Esme hugged herself to ward off the fever's chill. The pain in her temples grew stronger. Maybe this hadn't been a trap. Maybe this had been a test. Yes, the Nachtfrau wanted a report on the girl's magical skills for herself. If it was a test, had she passed?

The woman lit the small lantern on her belt, placed it on the ground next to Esme, and removed her hood. Three long braids spilled down her back. When Esme looked up into her rescuer's eyes for the first time, she started. The left half of the woman's face was hidden behind a mask of tailor-made glass. But when Esme peered at it closer, she saw it wasn't a mask. The left half of her face *was* glass. The edges blended seamlessly with the flawless light-olive flesh on the right side.

Noticing the girl's concern, the woman held up her left arm. It, too, was made of the same sparkling crystal. But her fingers flexed and her joints moved as if they didn't know they weren't flesh.

"A fascinating story, this. Maybe I'll tell you on the way to Somber End," she said. Before the girl could protest, the woman added, "If you still don't feel you need my assistance, I'll take my leave once we reach the village. Unless, of course, you haven't recovered yet. You don't appear in any condition—"

"I said I'm fine!" Esme leapt to her feet and almost immediately came crashing down again. She couldn't catch herself in time.

"I'm not going anywhere with you," she said, spitting sand from her mouth.

As the woman held out a hand, Esme rolled away, out of her reach.

"Your mother warned me you were stubborn."

"The fact that you follow her tells me I don't want you around. I don't even know who you are."

Esme tried to force herself up onto all fours again, but her arms didn't have the strength. Her head swam, assaulted by fever and a throbbing that had become unbearable. Even now, she could feel herself slipping away into unconsciousness.

"All you need to know is that the Nachtfrau sent me. My name is Birgit Freund . . ."

It was the last thing Esme heard before the fever took her.

13

The Margrave's Bargain

"THIS ISN'T POSSIBLE!"

Empress Sabine's every word was confident and pointed. Some, who didn't spend much time in her presence, confused this demeanor for anger. But on those rare occasions—such as now—when the empress was *clearly* angry, there was no mistaking it.

Guntram watched Sabine pace near the entrance of the royal healer's sanctum, deep in the imperial palace. Outside, the storm summoned by the Maiden raged on, loud and unstoppable. It felt as if even the palace's steadfast walls wouldn't be enough to protect them.

The prince's personal guards stood nearby, heads

bowed as they recounted what had happened in Somber End.

"I'm sorry, Your Majesty," Uwe said. "We saw it for ourselves. Everyone in Somber End saw it. The prince woke the Maiden. She came to life and attacked the village. She nearly killed the Margrave."

Guntram reclined on a slab as the healer tended to his wounds. The Maiden's flail had dug deep gashes into his left cheek, his chest, and thigh. The healer gently applied a thick green gel to his face. "This will help with the pain," he said to Guntram, "but there will be quite a scar."

Guntram didn't care about a scar. He couldn't even feel any pain. The terror that was coursing through his veins had left him numb to everything but his anger. Everything in his life could be taken away at any second as long as Alphonsus lived. The prince alone knew that Guntram had tried to kill him. The Margrave didn't need a clock—running backward or forward—to remind him that time was running out. He had to make sure the prince never had a chance to reveal what he knew. It helped that Somber End had turned against the boy. But Guntram was lost without additional leverage.

Despite Uwe's account, the empress persisted in her disbelief. "I don't doubt the Maiden is capable of violence.

But not my son. He would never knowingly harm anyone."

Tomas stepped forward. "Majesty, clearly sorcery is involved. When the ground shook, a clock was revealed in the statue's chest."

For the first time since learning of the Maiden's awakening, the empress appeared truly shaken. "A *what*?"

"A clock," Tomas repeated. "It was running backward. And when the prince went to awaken her, he, too, had a clock in his chest."

Guntram's eyes narrowed as he watched Sabine process this news. The empress had been shocked to hear about the Maiden's clock. But she hadn't so much as blinked to hear her son also had a clock in his chest.

She knew, Guntram realized. She already knew the boy had a clock. But how, if the Maiden's had only just been revealed . . . ?

Of course. The boy's clock wasn't new information. He'd had a clock . . . for how long? Since birth, perhaps? It didn't matter. The empress knew about her son's clock. And she'd never told anyone.

All at once, it felt like the sky had fallen on Guntram. The prince and the Maiden had shared a connection for a very long time, it seemed. Which meant the Maiden had been *using* Guntram, biding her time—and wasting his—until the prince came to her.

Guntram winced as the healer started sewing up the gash on his thigh. "Your Majesty," he said, speaking for the first time since returning from Somber End, "I think we can all agree that, whether or not the prince willfully knew what he was doing—"

"He did *not!*" Sabine insisted.

Guntram nodded respectfully. "I think we can all agree that backward-running clocks are not a good sign."

The empress stared past Guntram, her eyes fixed on the wall. She seemed miles away, as though kidnapped by thought. "'A sacrifice is all that saves,'" she whispered, "'the counterclockwise heart . . .'"

The Margrave's head tilted to one side. What was that about?

Before he could ask, the door to the healer's sanctum opened and Gerwalta, the captain of the royal guard, entered. She bowed low to the empress. "Majesty, my troops stand ready for your command. We are ready to pursue the Maiden, but the storm is too fierce. We must wait for it to pass before—"

"You will give chase immediately," the empress said. "We cannot allow them to get far."

Gerwalta stiffened. "Majesty, be reasonable. The Maiden was last seen going into the Hinterlands. That presents a whole other danger. Even if we catch up with them, we have no way to defeat the Maiden. Past attempts to harm her proved impossible. If we attack blindly, we cannot guarantee the prince's safety."

Guntram watched the empress seethe, torn between her protective nature and the captain's logic. A plan started to form in his mind. *Yes.* Yes, finally he could see a way out. He could deal with the prince, dispatch the Maiden, and, if all went well, gain more than he'd ever dared to dream.

As the healer finished stitching his leg, Guntram sat up. "The captain is right, Empress Sabine. There will be no one to rescue the prince if your own soldiers are in danger. When the storm has passed, they will be better able to deal with whatever perils the Hinterlands present."

Sabine whirled on him. "And what do we do while we wait out the storm? The captain just said we can't defeat the Maiden."

Guntram eased himself up to standing. "Majesty, I think the time has come to deal with the Maiden once and for all." He reached down, retrieved the prince's satchel from the floor, and removed two large chunks of onyx from within. "I'm sure Your Majesty is aware that diamonds are the hardest known substance. And just as it takes a diamond to cut another diamond"—he lifted one piece of onyx in his right hand and smashed it into the piece in his left, shattering the second piece—"so will the Maiden's onyx destroy itself. We use these pieces the prince gathered from the Maiden to craft weapons capable of grinding the statue to dust."

Sabine, who'd spent the last hour with an impenetrable expression on her face, let her guard down. She liked this idea, he could tell.

"I only hope," Guntram said, "that once the Maiden is defeated and the prince is safely home, the people don't continue to see him as a threat. It remains to be seen if the clock in his chest can be removed. If it's permanent, I don't see the people standing for that . . ."

Now, his brain was racing, calculating every possible move. Sabine regarded him coolly. He could see she'd reached exactly the conclusion that he'd hoped. She knew that he—Guntram—could reach the people of Somber End. They would listen to their longtime guardian. He, alone, could save her son. And, if they acted quickly, word of the prince wouldn't spread to the rest of the empire. As long as this news was contained to a single village—Somber End—the empress could ensure her son's safety.

"I wish to speak to the Margrave alone," Sabine said for all to hear. Everyone left the room.

"Empress," the Margrave said quickly, "I only meant—"

"The prince is not in league with the Maiden," the empress insisted. She sounded firm and resolute as always. But also, there was something else in her voice. Fear, maybe?

"I pray Your Majesty is correct, but the clock—"

"The clock isn't important."

Guntram nodded. "I believe that you believe that, Majesty. But you must understand, what I believe and what your subjects in Somber End believe are, at present, two different things."

"What do you mean?"

Guntram chose his next words carefully. "The people have believed for ten years that the Maiden will be their doom. They feel only hatred toward her. They have seen the clock in her chest, and they have seen the clock in your son. The damage is done. Everyone already links the prince to the Maiden. What remains to be seen is whether he is under her thrall . . . or she under his."

The empress scoffed. "How could anyone think that Alphonsus—"

"The boy was discovered in the palace walls *the very day* the Maiden appeared. How no one has connected the two events before now is a minor miracle in itself." Emboldened, he leaned in. "And yet people are making that connection as you and I speak. A connection that feels irrefutable.

"Once the storm passes, it won't be long until they are found. The Maiden moves surprisingly swiftly, given her size. But your army is efficient. They *will* catch her. They'll lay siege to her. But they'll only possess a small number of onyx weapons. If they fail to harm her, their attentions will turn to the prince . . ."

Sabine's eyes flared. "No one would *dare*."

"Fear makes people do terrible things. It robs them of reason. Everyone—even your own guards—are terrified of what the Maiden might do. Most will act before thinking. To them, this is a war. War takes the innocent and guilty alike. And even if we manage to rescue the prince, what about the people of Somber End? They believe he's been marked by the Maiden. They won't be easy to mollify. What will you do if your own people can't trust you?"

And there it was. Just what he'd been looking for. What he'd been working toward. *Doubt.* He saw it in her face. The smallest chip in her steadfast confidence. She didn't know how to save her son. She wasn't convinced it was even possible.

She was now ready to promise anything. *Do* anything.

"In the end, Majesty, I want what you want. I want Rheinvelt to be safe."

"I want my son to be safe."

"What if I told you both were possible?"

"How?"

"Send *me* with your soldiers. Put me in charge of the rescue mission."

The empress looked skeptical. "You mean well, Margrave, but you aren't qualified to lead a battalion."

Guntram laid his hand gently on Sabine's. "You brought me to the palace as an advisor. And there is nothing in the land I am more qualified to advise you on than the Maiden. Who knows her better than I? Who better to return your beloved son to you?"

Little by little, his words wore at her. She was ready to believe anything he told her. And Guntram was just getting started.

"I will direct all tactical maneuvers and make sure no harm comes to young Alphonsus," he pledged. "When we've safely returned him home, I can convince the people of Somber End that he was being controlled by the Maiden and that we still might save him. They'll listen to me, their guardian. They will be happy to hear that their future emperor is not beyond help."

Sabine bowed her head wearily. The fight had gone from her eyes. She'd lost confidence in her ability to quell the fear in her people. "Then do it. Do whatever it takes so no one harms Alphonsus. Return him to the palace, and you can name your reward. Money? Land? Whatever I can grant is yours. Just bring back my son."

Guntram waved his hand modestly. "Serving you, Majesty, will always be its own reward," he said, working not to betray his own eagerness. "And yet, I daresay that few have offered such service to the empire in the past. Vanquishing the greatest threat ever seen *and* returning the prince unharmed? Some might think impossible tasks like these cannot be compensated by mere riches."

If Sabine found his ambition impertinent, she didn't show it. No, she was far too focused on seeing her son safely returned. When she said she would do *anything* to get Alphonsus back, she meant it. And so the Margrave chose to ask for *everything*.

"Wealth and land can be fleeting, Your Majesty. If I do for you all I say, I require a reward far more enduring. Your hand, for example." He took a deep breath and looked the empress right in the eye. "In marriage."

PART TWO

It roared.

The sound—like steel grating on steel, the moans of a dying bear, and a monstrous gale combined—reverberated throughout the canyon. The roar echoed and diminished until it was gone. But nothing alive that heard the sound would soon forget it. Even as the cacophony diminished, the terror the roar had inspired lingered. This was not a roar of pain or anger. It was a cry of longing. The worst kind of longing. The creature roared because it didn't understand what it was longing for.

It had no legs, so it could not shamble. It had no arms, so it could not lumber. Yet it made its way through the barren Hinterlands. To all who observed it, the creature would not seem to be alive. Most would mistake it for a sandstorm, a ball-shaped whirlwind of sand tendrils and living shadows that churned in on themselves. But the creature moved. And it thought. And it felt. And this—these wastelands—were its domain.

For ten years, it had wandered the Hinterlands. It searched for something it didn't understand.

Its entire existence seemed to center on chasing a dream, always on the cusp of remembering whatever it was that it wanted. Almost remembering but failing. It hated the living. It hated the dead. It could abide neither. Where it encountered one, it sought to create the other. Somehow, it sensed, this would give it purpose. This would help it understand why it wandered the forsaken canyon. It had been a long time since the creature had had a chance to kill. Or to resurrect. It grew restless. It scoured its domain. Seeking, seeking, seeking.

It roared.

14

Memories,
Lost and Found

THE SOUND OF DISTANT THUNDER PULLED ESME FROM sleep. She had heard more thunder recently than ever before. It had become a new companion, so constant it felt married to her dreams.

She rubbed her eyes and, for the first time in quite a while, summoned the strength she needed to sit up. Light was scarce. Twilight? Dawn? Hard to say. She could just make out being surrounded by piles of massive stones. Each breath brought the scent of dry air and dust and a hint of smoke. Her last clear memory was of being in a canyon. Clearly, she was still there.

Esme fought to concentrate. Her recent memories were fuzzy at best. She remembered facing off against

the creatures in the canyon. She remembered being rescued by the mysterious huntress who worked for the
Nachtfrau. And . . . that was it.

Her body spent from the Balance of using so much
magic, she had drifted in and out of sleep that teemed
with the familiar dream of her father. She knew she had
woken at least twice to find Birgit Freund gently holding her head and spooning an earthy-tasting broth into
her mouth. But both times, Esme lacked the energy to
remain awake. Instead, she returned to the dream.

Now, though, the young Hierophant felt revitalized.
She felt stronger physically, her mind buzzing. Visions
from her dream continued even now that she was awake.
She realized two things immediately.

First, she no longer needed to use magic to induce
sleep and bring the dream of her father. It had come each
and every time she'd fallen asleep, replaying over and over.
The few times she woke and drank some of Birgit's broth
were mere pauses. The dream restarted exactly where it
had left off. She had now seen the visions so many times
that they were burned into her memory.

Second, the dreams were much more intense than
they'd ever been before. So real, so vibrant. She was convinced she could still smell the scent of her father—ginger
and honey—lingering in the air. She wasn't even sure
how she knew that was exactly how Klaus smelled. But

she knew. And just now, she awoke chilled, even though the air around her was humid and warm. Still, she felt as if she'd just come from the frozen North Lands, where the dream took place. The dream no longer felt detached and distant. Each time, she felt like she was really there.

This made Esme happy. She had barely known her father. She vaguely remembered him teaching her about the natural world. Her first words as a toddler were the names of the birds in the North Lands. He'd taught her about gemstones, his strongest passion outside the practice of magic. Even though she had been very young when he died, she'd held on to these dim memories like treasures.

Now, these vivid dreams made her feel closer than ever to Klaus, as though he, too, had made the journey to Rheinvelt. Esme could remember exactly how it felt when her dream father brushed her cheek with his hand. She swore that her other memories of her father were stronger now as well.

Of course, now that she was properly awake, those comforts gave way to the burden of the task ahead of her: removing the heart of the Onyx Maiden. Not to mention that *other* task that had brought her to Rheinvelt in the first place.

"Feeling better?"

Esme cleared her thoughts as Birgit emerged from the shadows. The remains of a small campfire smoldered behind the half-glass woman. Overhead, in a sky streaked with long gray clouds, Esme could see stars appearing.

Birgit knelt at Esme's side, causing the girl to flinch. "Well," Birgit said, "you're certainly *looking* better. I was worried. I can't remember the last time *I* slept for two days straight."

Esme leapt to her feet with a start. "Two days?" And although she felt better, the sudden movement proved too much. Dizziness invaded, and she was forced to grab the nearest rock for stability.

"Easy," Birgit warned. "I'd much rather we continue walking together than me carrying you."

Esme cursed silently to herself. Two days she'd been asleep. How could she allow that to happen when she knew time was of the essence? Every day she spent away from her people risked more Hierophants dying. If she'd just killed the Nachtfrau like she was supposed to, this would all have been over. But now she had no choice but to see this ridiculous mission through: find the Onyx Maiden and retrieve the statue's heart.

"I'm ready to go," Esme announced. "Which way is Somber End?"

Esme spun her head side to side, as if doing so would make the village suddenly appear. The huntress stood her ground, frowning.

"You might remember," Birgit said, "that I cared for you these past two days?"

"I didn't ask you to do that," Esme snapped. "I'm a Hierophant. I can take care of myself. I would have been fine without you."

Birgit didn't argue. Instead, she pointed to a nearby wall of rock that ran to the east as far as the eye could see. "See that ledge? We need to get up there. Are you strong enough to climb?"

"Yes, of course." Esme was highly skilled at climbing the icy fjords back home. A mere rock face would be simple.

With great care, she pulled herself up, higher and higher, until she stood on the ledge. Birgit soon followed.

"Now what?" Esme asked.

"Walk along the ledge. We'll follow as far as it goes," Birgit said.

"I thought we were coming up here to get our bearings," Esme said, frowning. "You're wasting time. It makes no sense to travel up here. The ledge is narrow. Using it will slow us down. We'll cover more ground if we go back down—"

Esme paused as she looked down at the walls of the canyon below. Even in the dying sunlight, she could just barely make out the dark outlines of mammoth sigils—four times as tall as Esme herself and as wide as a small stream—carved deep into the rock face. She studied them intently. Her magical studies with the Hierophant Collective had taught her hundreds and hundreds of sigils and the cants for each. But she had no idea what these symbols meant. They had been no part of her training, which seemed impossible. And even so, they looked familiar . . .

These were the sigils from her dream. The ones that glowed and sparkled in the sky just over her head as she and her father danced in a field of ice and snow. She'd been having that dream for as long as she could remember, but this was the first time she could recall exactly what the sigils looked like while she was awake. And now, here they were, carved deep into the canyon wall.

She reached her hand over the ledge and pressed her palm to the rocks. She could feel magic thrumming through the stone, a tickle that danced across her flesh. The spells she and every Hierophant cast—tracing symbols in the air and speaking their cants—was one kind of magic. To carve a glyph into an object and invoke its power was something altogether different. It was the most potent enchantment in the world. One that the Collective itself only rarely dared to wield.

This place was significant. It had to be. But what did it mean?

"Where are we?" Esme asked.

The huntress had started rummaging in the satchel on her hip. "The Hinterlands."

"Yes, I know that. Where in the Hinterlands? What is this place?"

"The Hinterlands are just . . . the Hinterlands. They're mostly unexplored by Rheinvelt. The imperial family has ancient maps, but it's hard to say how accurate they are."

In just these past few moments, the evening light had disappeared enough so that Esme could no longer see the symbols in the rocks. Still, she now remembered them clearly. Did this suggest her dream was, in some way, magical? Was it some sort of message her father had left behind? A special memory meant to lead her here?

No. Of course not. Her father had died when Esme was almost three. How could he have known the Collective would send her back to Rheinvelt? But she couldn't shake the feeling there was a connection.

Birgit pulled a copper spyglass from her satchel, extended it to full length, and directed it to the east.

"What are you looking for?" Esme asked.

Birgit frowned. "Something that's not there . . ." She handed the spyglass to the young Hierophant. In the distance, Esme saw the silhouette of a huge palace rising up above the dark tree line of the distant forest.

"I see a palace. What's not there?"

"See the tallest tower? There should be two lanterns hanging in the window. One green, one blue."

Esme focused on the tower. The window was dark. "So? There's nothing there. What does that mean?"

"It means something is wrong, but I . . ." Birgit paused. For the first time since meeting the huntress, Esme saw uncertainty in the woman's face. Birgit seemed confused and maybe just a little . . . scared. "Every night, I turn my spyglass to the palace, looking for those lights."

"Why?"

Birgit's human hand crossed over and touched the glass side of her face. "You see, that's the problem. I don't remember why. I just know it's something I'm supposed to do . . ."

Esme eyed the huntress. It was strange to perform the same task every night without knowing why. She started to wonder if she really was safe traveling with a woman who didn't seem to have complete control over her memories.

Birgit pointed to the palace in the distance. "For the last year, the lights have always been there. Every single night for a year. And I've known somehow that means all is well. But there have been *no* lights in the tower for the past two nights, and I know that's bad. I know it means *something* . . . but I can't remember what."

The human half of Birgit's face scowled as if in pain,

while the glass half hardly moved at all. Esme watched her struggle for this forgotten knowledge for a moment, then the huntress shrugged it off.

"We have a duty," Birgit said. "Best be on our way."

Together, they took gingerly steps along the ledge, hugging the canyon wall for support. The path was slick with moss, and Esme nearly slipped twice.

"It's dangerous up here," the young Hierophant said. "It would be safer on the ground."

Birgit shook her head. "It rained while you were asleep. The muddied ground makes us easier to track. We can better hide our movements if we stick to the ledge as long as possible."

"Is hiding our movements really important?"

"Very," Birgit said. "We're being hunted."

15

Fire and Steel and Onyx

THE WEAPON FOUNDRIES BURIED DEEP BENEATH THE IMPERIAL palace spat fire like a dragon come to life with one purpose: vengeance. Great billows stoked the flames that kept the metal red-hot and ready to be fashioned into anything Guntram demanded. And with his abundant imagination, the Margrave had amassed an arsenal unlike any seen in the empire's history.

The relentless heat of the forge was a welcome respite from the cold winds and driving rains that had plagued the imperial palace the past two days. Since being placed in charge of the battalion that was to seek out and destroy the Onyx Maiden, Guntram had spent most of his time here. He consulted with the smiths every hour, collaborating on the size and shape of every weapon. He also inspected each finished weapon, once it had been affixed with onyx. As far as anyone could tell, the onyx itself looked ordinary. This may have been true, but Guntram believed it held great power.

It was a cunning plan, of course. Guntram was quite pleased with himself. He'd had many cunning plans of late. *Emperor Guntram.* He loved how it rang in his ears when he spoke it aloud in private. Almost as much as he'd loved hearing Sabine's promise to marry him when this was all over. A promise, he was eternally happy to remind himself, that would bring him the ultimate power he sought. And it came with a very clever loophole.

"Destroy the Maiden and bring my son to me," Empress Sabine had said before an assembly of the imperial court's lords and ladies to make her decree formal, "and we shall be wed, to rule the empire as husband and wife."

In her haste to rescue her son from the Maiden, the empress had never stipulated that the prince must return *alive.*

Guntram felt confident that, in the chaos of battle, it would be fairly easy to slip through the lines and put an end to Alphonsus. He'd be considered a casualty of war. All would swear they'd done their best to protect him. And when the empress finished mourning, Guntram would remind her of her promise. He would be emperor of all.

"You should get some rest, Margrave."

Guntram turned to find Empress Sabine following behind him, inspecting each blade in turn. Even as she held a sword up to the light, twirling it with the agility of any seasoned warrior, he could tell she was watching him.

"Indeed, Majesty," Guntram said with a small bow. "The days ahead will prove to be dangerous."

The empress nodded. "We are so very fortunate to have your counsel in this grave matter."

Guntram turned his head quickly to prevent the empress from seeing the involuntary smirk on his face when she said "grave matter." An image of himself driving an onyx blade into the prince's chest flashed in his mind, and it filled him with joy.

He'd been so lost in this new thought he'd missed that the empress was still talking.

"We have much to do until we find the Maiden."

Guntram nodded. "Yes, Majesty. I will work hard to track down the Maiden and your son as you tend to matters here at the palace. I've arranged for messengers to join our party so that I might send you regular missives on our progress—"

The empress laughed. "Don't be ridiculous, Margrave. That won't be necessary. I have appointed Lady Adalheid to lead in my stead. It is she who will be sending messengers to us."

The Margrave pressed his hand against the armory wall to steady himself. "Lady Adalheid? I don't understand, Your Majesty."

"Margrave," Sabine said, a playful lilt in her voice, "an empress cannot take just any consort as her husband. Any potential emperor must prove his worth as a leader. If you are to be my husband and rule at my side, I need to see evidence of your valor, your discretion under the strains of battle."

The empress pulled back the front of the robe she wore, revealing an armored breastplate that shone of gold and chrome. Then she selected the largest broadsword she could find, slid it skillfully into a scabbard around her waist, and smiled at the Margrave.

"I'm coming with you."

Once the empress had retired for the evening, Guntram stepped outside the palace into the courtyard gardens. The rain had only just stopped, but it was still cold and windy. Nonetheless, he marched through the shoulder-high rosebushes, stopped just out of sight of the palace entrance, and vomited on the ground.

What did Sabine mean she was joining the mission?

There was no way he could make the prince's death look like an accident with her around. Worse, Sabine's presence made it easier for the prince to reveal what had happened between him and the Margrave in the throne room. Which made it very likely Guntram would die before he had the pleasure of watching the Maiden fall.

He decided to run. He would go to his apartments, pack what he could, and travel south to the misty rain forests that lay beyond Rheinvelt's farthest border. It was a land of wild animals, lethal plants, and rivers that boiled, but there were no monarchs who would gladly turn him over to the empress.

He turned to leave the hedge maze and found an armored silhouette blocking his path. Believing he'd already been exposed and was now being arrested, Guntram cried out.

"Sorry to frighten you, Margrave," the soldier said. His helmet bore the insignia of the imperial family: a green hawk soaring over a blue river. "Captain Gerwalta assigned me to your protection. I was told to stay close."

Recognizing the voice, Guntram peered into the darkness. "I know you," Guntram said. "Otto. Right?"

They had known each other as children. Otto had been one of the mongrels in Somber End who'd mocked

Guntram for his tattered clothes. And then they'd mocked him for talking to a statue. Now, however, Otto's tone was quite contrite.

The soldier bowed his head. "I was . . . I was hoping you wouldn't remember, Margrave. I apologize for anything I may have said . . . I was just a boy. But now, I'm honored to be serving with you on this mission."

Guntram's stomach lurched with anger. Was this more mockery? Was he to spend the entire march into the Hinterlands enduring the laughing whispers of the soldiers around him?

"I don't know what you mean," Guntram said.

Otto laughed nervously. "Well . . . you're the guardian, sir. If anyone can save the prince and destroy the Maiden, it's you."

Guntram felt a warm tingle to hear his own arguments parroted back to him. It didn't matter that *he* didn't believe them. It only mattered that others thought it was true. And, obviously, others did.

The Margrave decided to test the waters. He held up his hands. "I'm no longer sure I'll be joining the mission. I feel I've contributed all I can in creating the onyx weapons. I'd only get in the way. You're the real soldiers. You don't need me."

Otto's jaw went slack. He stared dumbly at the

Margrave, shaking his head slowly. "I don't think you understand, Margrave. You are . . . Everyone thinks you . . . Come with me."

Otto led the Margrave across the courtyard to the barnlike building that served as barracks for the imperial army. They entered a great hall where men and women had gathered for their evening meal. As Otto led Guntram just inside the door, all conversations stopped. As one, the warriors laid their silverware down, stood, and bowed at the waist in the Margrave's direction.

Guntram knew most of them from Somber End. When the likes of Otto and most of the others in the room had come of age and joined the imperial army, Guntram had still been sitting at the Maiden's base and whispering his dreams to her. One of those dreams, strangely enough, had been to hold dominion over those who'd spent years insulting him. As angry as he was at the Maiden, Guntram realized that this small wish had been seemingly granted.

"Tomorrow, we serve our empress," Otto said, addressing the soldiers. "Gerwalta will command us in our quest. She is a smart and cunning leader." He turned to face the Margrave. "But *you* know the Maiden. You faced her down every day for over ten years. Every woman and man in this room would rather stand at your side in a battle against her than face her with anyone else."

Guntram bowed his head, pretending to be humbled. When he looked up again, everyone banged their fists on the long wooden tables in approval. Guntram had their fealty. How far would that loyalty go? Did their fear of the Maiden's wrath trump their oath of service to the empress?

There was an awkward pause. Guntram realized they were waiting for him to speak.

"I'm no soldier," the Margrave said slowly, searching for words. "I am only a humble advisor. I can share the knowledge I have of the Maiden and her treachery. Not even the seers who warned us of this day could have imagined that the Maiden would take possession of our beloved prince. I fear the worst for him. I fear he's become her servant and that all hope is lost. More than that, I fear the empress doesn't see that. She's a mother who loves her son. She's blinded by that love. She can't see that the boy who walks around with a clock in his chest is no longer her son. He's a pawn of the Maiden. A tool. Who knows what lies he might tell to gain our confidence? We must be vigilant in the days ahead. Beware of deception. Beware of those who have been compromised. Look to those you *know* you can trust."

The soldiers' applause shook the timbers that held up the stone roof. The desire to collect his belongings and run south bled from Guntram. He had hope.

There might be a way out of this yet.

16

When Nights Pass as Hours the Same . . .

BRRDA-TICK-CLICK! BRRDA-TICK-CLICK! BRRDA-TICK-CLICK!

As dusk settled in—the third dusk in the two days since fleeing Somber End—Prince Alphonsus huddled close to a small campfire in the Hinterlands. These deserts to the west of Rheinvelt were unlike anything he'd seen. Where his homeland teemed with life—blossoming trees, fertile fields of green, and glistening lakes and waterfalls—the Hinterlands were stark and unforgiving. The landscape had its own sense of beauty, he supposed. In their trek, he'd seen great valleys, bowls of earth made of rough sandstone with layers that passed from dark orange to light brown. They lent magnificence to an otherwise desolate place.

The deeper he and the Maiden had traveled into the Hinterlands, the scarcer food and water had grown. Nightly, they heard more and more howls and growls in the darkness. At noon, the punishingly hot temperatures made him glad he had only his breeches. But as twilight fell, he slept as close as he could to the campfire the Maiden made.

The prince sat hugging his knees at the base of the campfire. He shivered. Despite the frequent sun, they'd also encountered several rain showers. These would have been refreshing if the water hadn't been so hot. Then the temperatures dropped at night, leaving the prince cold. The fire allowed him to dry off . . . until it rained the next day.

The canyon they'd entered a day and a half ago had natural pathways carved through it. The Maiden boldly navigated them, taking lefts and rights, somehow knowing where she was going. Alphonsus never questioned it.

Tonight, all was silent, save the ticking of the twin clocks. He was sure it wasn't thundering nearly as loudly as he thought it was. Was it? To his ears, it certainly sounded that way. But lately, he'd found it difficult to tell what was real and what wasn't. Little felt real anymore.

Alphonsus knew just one thing for sure: for the first time in a very, very long time, he didn't feel afraid. He didn't worry about dying. He didn't worry about the clock in his chest running backward.

He'd forgotten what it was like to live without fear. He remembered now that it filled him with warmth. He'd missed that feeling.

He might have felt differently had he known that, just leagues away in the royal palace, Guntram Steinherz was marshaling an army meant to track down and destroy the Onyx Maiden (and kill the prince in the process). Or that, closer still, Esme Faust, the last Hierophant in Rheinvelt, was marching through the Hinterlands, intent on using her arcane powers to remove the Maiden's heart, which the prince now knew to be a clock much like his own. Had Alphonsus known these disparate forces were closing in on him, he might have felt terrified. At the moment, though, he had what he considered a far bigger problem.

"Fire."

Alphonsus pointed at the flames of their campfire and repeated the word: "Fire." The Onyx Maiden sat cross-legged, her back pressed to a rocky hill. The eternal scream on her face was gone, and she sat expressionless, watching Alphonsus try desperately to communicate.

She'd never spoken. For two days straight, she'd carried the boy on her shoulders, never uttering a sound once they'd left Somber End behind. For reasons Alphonsus couldn't explain, he trusted her. Even when she had carried him deep into the Hinterlands. Inhospitable and bleak, it seemed an odd choice for a place to seek refuge. And there was also the matter of the wasteland's mysterious inhabitants, whom they had yet to encounter. Then again, Alphonsus reasoned, the harsh conditions would make it harder for Guntram to follow him.

And though they'd never exchanged words, the Maiden somehow knew what the prince needed. When he felt hungry, she knew. She would stop and find him shelter under a copse of trees or in a cave. Then she'd disappear for a short while and return with nuts and berries or the occasional freshly killed rabbit for him to eat. When he felt tired, she knew. She would scoop out a massive handful of earth, lay him gently at the bottom of the shallow hole, and stand guard until he was well rested.

But though his needs were tended to without request, Alphonsus knew the pair wouldn't be able to accomplish much until they learned to communicate.

The Maiden regarded the prince blankly. No matter how often he jabbed his fingers toward the flames, she wouldn't say "fire." Still, the prince wasn't to be deterred.

He leaned back and thrust his foot into the air. "Foot!" he declared, pointing to the appendage. The Maiden tilted her head. It looked like she was at least *trying* to understand.

He smiled. "That's right. Can you say 'foot'? 'Foot'?" He kept pointing excitedly.

The Maiden lifted her free hand and began jabbing toward the sky with one finger. *"Foot!"*

Despite being made of precious stone, the voice that came from the Maiden's mouth sounded like the squeal of a thousand metal forks scraping against a thousand metal plates. It hurt the prince's teeth to hear it.

But she'd spoken!

Alphonsus shook his head. "No, no. *This* is a foot." He grabbed his whole foot with one hand and gestured to it with the other. "Foot!"

The Maiden mimicked his gestures, gripping a handful of empty air and poking the empty space with her other hand. *"Foot!"*

Alphonsus winced at the metallic screaming. Suddenly, communicating seemed less important. Especially if it came with pain. But if his mother had taught him anything, it was persistence. The two *needed* to be able to talk. And, if he was being honest, he needed someone to talk to.

He needed someone to tell him what to do next.

The prince raised his leg higher and grabbed his big toe. "Toe! Toe!" Perhaps "foot" had been too difficult?

This time, the Maiden leaned forward with a single finger—a finger three times as tall as Alphonsus and twice as thick—and tapped the boy's foot. As the mammoth statue touched Alphonsus, he flipped head over heels and flew back several feet, landing facedown. He lifted his head and glared at the Maiden. She stared back innocently.

"*Toe!*"

Sighing, the prince brushed himself off and returned to his seat near the fire. The Maiden looked at him as if she expected him to continue. Alphonsus shook his head. He wasn't sure he could survive another vocabulary lesson.

"Back in Somber End, I would imagine that you would come to life and we could talk," the prince said. "Not just you listening to me. But both of us talking. That's not going to happen, is it?"

The Maiden lowered her arm and hung her head.

"Still," Alphonsus said, studying her, "you *do* understand me, don't you?" He considered a moment, then traced the edge of his clock with a finger. "Clock. Clock." He pointed to the clock in the Maiden's chest.

She looked from his clock to her own, touched her chest, and said, "*Foot!*"

"We're the same," Alphonsus said. "How is that possible? Do you know how this happened?"

The Maiden paused. Leaning forward, she sank a huge finger into the earth and dragged it slowly, digging out a ditch as she did. She changed her finger's direction, curving it around twice before lifting her hand again.

She's drawing, the prince thought. He couldn't quite make out what it was, though.

Springing to his feet, Alphonsus ran to a small mound of rocks and scrambled his way to the top. From this height, he looked down at the Maiden's drawing. She'd traced the symbol of a heart.

"Yes," he said to her. "It's our heart."

The Maiden shook her head. She pointed to the heart she'd just drawn on the ground, then pointed to the clock in the prince's chest. She did this three times, each time getting a little bit closer to actually touching Alphonsus's clock. He didn't know what she was trying to say.

Alphonsus tapped his clock. "I was found in the palace walls as a baby. I don't know where this came from. I don't know where *I* came from."

At this, the Maiden stood. She looked around, as if to get her bearings. Then she lifted a mighty arm and pointed south.

"Toe!"

Alphonsus didn't understand. Was that where they were headed next? He hadn't questioned where she was leading them. He'd asked her for help, and she'd brought him here. Did she have a plan?

"What are you saying?" he asked. "Is there somewhere you want me to go?"

The Maiden pointed again to the prince's clock and then to the south. Alphonsus wished more than ever that they could talk to each other. He didn't understand . . .

Except . . . she'd started indicating south once he'd confessed that he didn't know where he'd come from.

"Is that where I come from?" he asked. "Do you know where I'm from?"

The Maiden gave a single solemn nod. *"Foot!"*

All other thoughts—of his encounter with Guntram, of the danger he'd left his mother in—vanished from the prince's mind. "Take me there!" Alphonsus declared. He kicked dirt over the fire until it was out and scurried around, collecting the food the Maiden had brought him. When he was ready, he stood expectantly, waiting for the statue to hoist him onto her shoulders.

But she didn't. Instead, she pointed west at the setting sun. Then she pointed up to the sky, already dark gray with stars peeking through. For someone who couldn't really talk, her message was clear. They were staying here for the night.

"All right," Alphonsus said with a sigh. As the Maiden carved away at the heart she'd drawn, making another shallow hole for the prince to sleep in, Alphonsus made his way to a nearby stream. He ladled handfuls of water into his mouth, his mind racing all the while about the possibility of learning where he came from in the morning.

That was when he remembered his mother. And Guntram. By now, he imagined, the Margrave's insurrection might be complete. Maybe he'd taken over the entire palace, consigned his mother to the dungeon. Or worse. No doubt, Guntram was spreading more lies, continuing to poison the minds of everyone in the land against the prince.

Tomorrow, that would change. If the Maiden was leading him to the person who placed the clock in his chest, then surely there were other people there too. People who could help Alphonsus. Tomorrow, he'd take steps to reclaim his empire.

The prince leaned over the stream and splashed its cool water on his face. He shivered, but it felt good. He gazed down at his reflection, attempting to summon the courage he would need to rally others to his side. Instead, he saw a coward gazing back. Then he noticed his clock.

The number 12 had disappeared from the face. So had 11. The clock continued to run, its thin second hand moving backward. The minute hand pointed down toward the 6, but the hour hand pointed up to where the 11 should be . . . and wasn't. He leaned forward, searching for scratch marks. Perhaps the numbers had been accidentally rubbed off during their journey. But no. The clockface was smooth and unblemished. It was as though the numbers had never existed.

He turned to look at the Maiden. Her clock had all twelve numbers. Whatever this was affected him alone. And while completely new and mysterious, it also seemed . . . familiar. Missing hours . . . missing hours . . .

As if summoned, the words of a long-forgotten rhyme seeped into the prince's mind.

"'When nights pass as hours the same . . .'" he whispered. How did the rest of it go? It had been so long since he'd read it on the underside of the bassinet, so long since his mother had dismissed it as meaningless. But the words were important; he was sure of it.

"'When nights pass as hours the same, the end of time will start.'" He spoke slowly, fighting to remember each word exactly as it had appeared. There was something else, something about being saved. How did it go? He remembered how it ended. *The counterclockwise heart.*

His heart.

Someone—whoever had carved the rhyme into the bassinet—had foreseen this. They'd known what would happen to Alphonsus.

Nights and hours were passing the same. Two days

since they'd fled Somber End. Two numbers—*hours*—missing from the clockface. With each day that continued to pass, he suspected another number would vanish. Like a countdown. What was less clear was what happened at the end of the countdown.

No. What he remembered of the rhyme told him exactly what would happen. *The end of time.*

He was going to die.

17

The Hunted

Dawn arrived, masked by surly gray clouds that roiled on the horizon. A new storm was approaching the Hinterlands.

Esme awoke to find Birgit lying stiffly beside her. They'd taken shelter for the night in a small alcove recessed into a rocky canyon wall. There was barely enough room for the pair of them. Clearly, Birgit had woken first but hadn't stirred.

"Is it safe to move?" Birgit asked.

Before going to sleep, Esme had cast a spell that shielded them from all living perception. Anything hunting them would be unable to see, hear, or smell them while under the spell's protection. For the spell to work, though, they had to remain in one spot. As soon as they broke camp, they'd be vulnerable.

Esme frowned. "Yes, of course it is." She cleared her throat. Her voice sounded hoarse and weak. Her hands were closed into fists. She couldn't move her fingers. Temporary paralysis of her hands. The Balance from last night's spell. Unable to draw sigils, she hoped she didn't need to use her magic before it wore off.

Birgit propped herself up on one elbow. "I wasn't sure. You said we couldn't move—"

"I said we had to stay close," Esme snapped, upset to be this impatient so early. "The spell has a limited range."

Birgit crawled over Esme and out of the alcove. She stood up and stretched. "We should find some breakfast and head out."

Esme stared at her in disbelief. "Would you like to tell me what's going on?"

"Sorry?"

"Last night, you said we're being hunted, then refused to talk about it. You said if we talked, whatever was hunting us would track us down. But you don't have any problems talking now."

Birgit laughed. "I said that because I was tired of talking. And I wanted you to be quiet for a while."

"You liar!" A thousand cants danced on Esme's tongue. If she could have used her hands, she'd have made Birgit's hair fall out. Or sewn her mouth shut. She knew a hundred different spells to teach the huntress a lesson. Instead, all she could do now was sputter. "This is all a trick. The Nachtfrau sent you to distract me, not help me. You lied about not talking, you lied about being hunted—"

"No," Birgit said gently, "that part is true. We are most definitely being hunted. Or we were, last night. It's possible that when you hid us with your magic, our hunter gave up. But nonetheless, we should proceed with caution."

Esme planted herself, fists on her hips. "No. I won't cower. I need to find the Maiden quickly and get this over with. I don't have time to hide from some . . . thing that's hunting us. We should stand and fight."

"You don't even know what's hunting us."

"I can handle it."

"You have a lot of confidence in your magical training."

"With good reason."

Birgit looked the young Hierophant up and down. "Interesting."

"What?"

"When you're not bragging about your magical powers or proving your magical superiority . . . I wonder who you are?"

Esme flinched. The words cut deep. "You're not making sense. I'm who I am, whether I use my magic or not."

"I don't think so. You've only ever known what it is to wield mystical abilities and bend any obstacle to your will. Have you ever considered the perspective of those of us who can't use magic? What we have to do to get by day to day?" The huntress studied her companion's face. "Who are you without your magic, Esme?"

The Hierophant's face flushed with anger and frustration. She wanted to lash out at Birgit and tell her exactly who she was.

But Esme didn't. Because she didn't have an answer.

"This is none of your business," she said coolly. "My magic—"

"Magic isn't always the answer. That's something your mother taught me."

Esme stomped over to Birgit and leaned in until they were nose to nose. "Stop. Calling. Her. My. Mother!"

Birgit didn't even blink. She stared the Hierophant down and calmly said, "She is your mother whether you say it or not."

Esme closed her eyes. She could feel her temper rising, clawing at her from the pit of her stomach. But no. This was all part of the Nachtfrau's plan. She wanted Esme to be angry. She wanted Esme to be distracted. Every moment Esme spent not focused on getting the Onyx Maiden's heart was a moment the Hierophants in the North Lands were suffering. She reminded herself that she had one goal: end the curse by any means necessary.

Feeling slowly returned to her fingers. She flexed them, and they reminded her of pale-white spiders. The Hierophant turned and gathered her supplies. "Go back to the Hexen Woods. I can do this on my own."

"Are you prepared to kill?"

A chill slid down Esme's back. She swallowed hard. "What?"

"If you're confronted by what's hunting us, are you prepared to kill?"

"Yes. If necessary."

"Really? Killing the creatures that attacked you when you first arrived in the Hinterlands would have been a simple solution. But it seems to me you couldn't quite bring yourself to do it."

Esme felt her cheeks flush. Her anger rumbled inside, but this time she was angry with herself. For being reluctant to kill. For allowing anyone to see that reluctance. "What do you know?" she spat.

"I'm a huntress. Killing is what I do. And you'll need me when our predator makes its move."

Esme growled. "Fine. You can come. But not because I refuse to kill what's hunting us. I don't want to waste my energy on that. I need to stay sharp for when we find the Onyx Maiden."

"Of course," Birgit said, with a little bow of her head. She turned and started marching south.

"Where are you going?" Esme asked.

Birgit nodded her head to the nearby mountain pass. "This way will afford us some protection if our ... 'friend' decides to come looking for us again."

"But Somber End is to the east."

"And the Maiden is to the south."

"The Nachtfrau said it was in Somber End."

"I'm an expert tracker. I'm telling you, that's no longer true."

Esme took a breath, ready to blast the huntress. Another deception! Clearly, Birgit had instructions from the Nachtfrau to lead Esme away from the Maiden and slow her down. But Esme stopped herself. Instead, she smiled broadly, reaching into her sack, and pulled out the infinitum box.

"Well," she said smoothly, "there's one way to know for sure." She opened the lid, her father's voice—it sounded different this time, a bit lighter than it had been in Esme's recent dream—spoke the rhyme, and Esme asked: "Where is the Onyx Maiden?"

The box wheezed, then said, "*The Maiden hides among the mountains at the eastern edge of Rheinvelt.*"

That was obviously the lie. Esme waited for the box to tell her that the Maiden was in Somber End. But the box paused. Esme thought it seemed longer than any other pause from the box. Then it said, *"The Maiden is nearing Silberglas."*

Impossible! Esme slammed the box's lid shut. "Did the Nachtfrau tell me a single truth? We're supposed to be going to a statue in Somber End. How could it move? Was it stolen?"

Birgit seemed less concerned with the news that the statue wasn't where they'd been told and more concerned with how they might get to where it now was. "If the Maiden's in the mountains," she said, "we're several days away. But if she's in Silberglas, we're quite close. Silberglas is here, in the Hinterlands." With a grin, the huntress lifted her glass arm and pointed. "To the *south*."

Without a word, Birgit turned and headed that way. Esme ran to catch up with her.

"So where are we going? What is Silberglas?"

Birgit raised an eyebrow. "You don't know? Interesting. I'd never heard of it either until your mother sent me to help you. She called it 'the secret city of the Hierophants.'"

Esme laughed. "There's no such thing. Not here in the Hinterlands, anyway. The Hierophants lived in the mountains when they lived in Rheinvelt."

"Yes, they did. But I think the important word there

is 'secret.' They had a city here in the Hinterlands that they didn't want anyone to know about."

Esme scoffed. But then she remembered the previous day, when she saw the huge glyphs carved into the canyon walls. The mysterious symbols she'd never seen before. Obviously, the Hierophants *had* been here. But what was the purpose of the secret city?

And, more important, why had the Collective never told her about it?

Somewhere to the east, a crack of thunder rent the sky. As if in answer, a great roar sounded behind them. Distant, but fierce and terrifying. It had come from something alive. Something big. It was unlike anything Esme had ever heard. A second roar, more powerful than the last, sent gooseflesh racing up and down her arms.

"I think," Birgit said slowly, "we have a race on our hands. Can we get to Silberglas before what's hunting us arrives?"

18

Monster

Alphonsus woke the next morning to the sound of small children laughing and whispering.

He stirred at the bottom of the trench that the Maiden had dug for him to sleep in. "Hello?" he called out. The only response was more giggling and the sound of someone scampering away. The prince crawled out of the hole, looked around, and found no one.

Not even the Maiden.

Alphonsus scaled the tallest rock he could find, his head whipping around wildly as he searched in every direction. But the tall canyon walls revealed little beyond the gulley in which they'd set up camp the previous night. Since they'd fled Somber End three days ago, the Maiden had never left his sight. He'd looked to the statue for protection. Not once had he been afraid while she was near. Now, she was gone without explanation.

But he wasn't alone.

Alphonsus peered around slowly, studying the rock formations along the canyon walls. He could feel his old companion—fear—creeping around in his stomach. "Is someone there? You don't have to be afraid."

He didn't know if he was speaking to the whispers that seemed to come from all around or if he was saying it to himself. If the latter, it wasn't working.

Alphonsus lowered into a crouch and picked up a rock to use as a weapon. Every lesson he'd learned from Birgit Freund—how to hunt, how to fight—tumbled through his mind. Even so, he couldn't ignore the terror that, as always, kept him from focusing.

"Come out!" he demanded, trying to sound like a prince.

It worked.

A small boy, about half the prince's size, peeked out from behind a cone-shaped rock. The boy had long, shaggy blond hair and skin so pale it was almost the color of bone. His eyes widened as he looked at Alphonsus, and he broke into a wide grin.

The prince felt a wave of relief. "Hello. Who are you?"

The little boy giggled and disappeared behind the

rock. A moment later, a young girl—the boy's sister?—poked her head up over the same stone. She had the same beautiful smile as the boy. They looked almost identical except she was missing her right eye. In its place sat a multifaceted emerald that sparkled when she gazed at the prince. Yes, the prince decided, they must be brother and sister.

Alphonsus knelt and smiled back. He waved them over. "I won't hurt you. Come over here where I can see you better."

The girl ducked down, and Alphonsus could hear them both laugh. Then, slowly, each child came out from behind the stone. Now that he could see the boy fully, Alphonsus noted he was missing his left leg. A small garden hoe, fastened to his hip with hinges and wire, allowed the child to walk with only the slightest limp.

"My name is Alphonsus," the prince said. "Where are your parents? What are you doing in the Hinterlands? Do you live here?"

The children approached with tentative steps, smiling all the while. The girl made it to Alphonsus first. She seemed fixated by the clock in his chest (which, Alphonsus noticed, was now missing the number 10). She touched the emerald in her face, then touched the face of the prince's clock.

Alphonsus took out the small sack he'd been carrying since leaving Somber End and emptied out what little food he had left. "Go on. Help yourselves. Are you hungry?"

The children ignored the food. Instead, the boy followed his sister's lead. He touched the hoe that acted as his leg, then touched the clock. "Leichleben," the boy said in a high-pitched voice.

Alphonsus squinted, not sure what the word meant. "It's my heart," he said. "I guess. I'm not really sure."

As the children continued to run their fingers over the clockface, Alphonsus tried to redirect them to the food. He scooped up a handful of berries and pretended to eat them. But when he offered the berries to the children, they still didn't take any.

And that's when it occurred to him. He was the same as these children. They all three had something that stood in for part of their bodies. He remembered the Maiden suggesting she could show Alphonsus where he came from. Were these two from that place? Was it far?

The prince quickly gathered the food back into his sack and took the children by the hand. "We're going to play a game," he told them. "You're going to show me where you live."

The children gleefully pulled Alphonsus toward a

path where the canyon walls split into a fork. Alphonsus looked for the Maiden's footprints or any sign as to where she'd gone. But there wasn't a trace.

The children were about to lead Alphonsus down the right fork when an unearthly shriek, accompanied by a burst of wind, pushed in from their path. The children yelped and scuttled to hide behind Alphonsus, who put his arms out, as if to shield them from whatever had made that horrible sound.

"What was that?" Alphonsus asked. Since they'd entered the Hinterlands, he'd heard the howls of various unseen beasts in the night. But nothing like that. This sound, like the Maiden's voice, hurt his teeth.

Whatever it was, the children knew it instantly. The boy wrapped his arms around one of the prince's legs. The girl used her brother as a ladder, climbed onto Alphonsus's shoulders, and whispered a single word.

"Monster."

The terrible shriek rang out again, this time much louder . . . and definitely closer. The children cried and buried their faces in Alphonsus.

"Listen," he said gently, lowering the girl to the ground next to her brother. "I don't think we should be here when it arrives. I have a friend who can help us . . . If we can find her. I'm not sure where she—"

Another horrific howl. There was no time to wonder further where the Maiden had gone. Alphonsus once again grabbed the children by the hand, and together they ran.

The still-glowing coals of a campfire smoldered. The creature stopped to investigate.

Yes. Something had been here. Something living. Something it had been hunting for some time now. Something that needed to die.

It immediately regretted this urge. Why did it want to kill? It always felt sad afterward. It always tried to make amends. Often, though, it was too late.

The creature's tendrils of sand and debris flicked about wildly, extinguishing the remains of the fire. It didn't like to think about its feelings. Its existence was better when it was neither happy nor sad. Nor anything. It just wanted to be. That was enough.

And yet it was never enough.

Then: The sound. The word. The name.

The creature heard very little. Often, the cacophony of its own thrashing and churning drowned out all other sounds. But it had a gift. There was one thing it could hear above all else. No matter the clamor, no matter how quietly it was whispered, it could always hear its name.

"Leichleben."

Whenever, wherever its name was uttered, everything seemed to stand still. That one word could pierce through any tumult, over any distance.

The creature didn't like others using its name. Names, it knew, were power. And no one would have power over the creature. Not again.

It roared. It screamed.

With a surge, it thundered its way through the canyon, searching for whoever dared speak its name.

The speaker would be silenced.

19

Warn the Prince

"IT'S A CANYON."

Esme had seen plenty of canyons. Granted, the ones she'd seen were back in the North Lands and were carved into glaciers of ice. But made from stone or ice, a canyon was a canyon.

They'd climbed a tall, thin mesa splitting their path. "This will help us see where we are," Birgit had reasoned aloud. So they'd scaled to the mesa's flat top, high above the gorge, all to learn what they'd already known.

"It's a canyon," Esme repeated. "I thought you were taking me to 'the secret city.'"

"We can see the whole canyon from here," Birgit said.

"Did the Collective teach you nothing of how to find your way? Knowing exactly where we are will help us find Silberglas."

Esme grunted her disapproval. She'd come to hate it here. In the North Lands, with her fellow Hierophants, she felt confident. Her magical skills were unquestioned. She lived by the word of the Collective. Except for the harsh conditions that threatened the lives of everyone she knew, her life was nearly perfect.

But leaving home had changed all that. Everything about her journey challenged what she thought she knew. As she performed increasingly complex magic, she found herself facing Balances she couldn't have anticipated. This made her reluctant to try new things as she questioned her strength. The Nachtfrau hadn't proved nearly as forbidding as the terrible stories Esme had heard. She knew—the Collective had *told* her—what a monster her mother was. But still, Esme's every instinct screamed that things with the Nachtfrau weren't quite as cut-and-dried as she'd believed.

And then there was the Collective itself. Her teachers—the ones who'd trusted her with their most powerful secrets, who'd trained her with abilities that surpassed all other Hierophants in the North Lands—had not, it seemed, been completely honest. Despite telling Esme that she'd mastered all known sigils, there were those symbols carved into the other canyon's walls that remained a mystery.

In so many ways, it felt as though everything Esme had ever believed in was now in question. And she hated that feeling. She'd always had faith that her mastery of magic could solve any problem she encountered. But this problem, it seemed, had no magical solution.

Who are you without your magic? Birgit's question had come back to haunt and taunt her.

With a beleaguered sigh, Esme surveyed the land below. She could see the canyon for what it was: a natural labyrinth of dry riverbeds that coursed through the walls of brown and red stone as far as the eye could see.

Birgit pulled out her spyglass and held it to her human eye. She stared north, muttered to herself, then turned west and said, "Oh."

"Do you see Silberglas?"

"Not exactly."

Birgit handed the spyglass to the young Hierophant. Esme drew a bead on the spot the huntress had been looking and turned the end of the spyglass until a lengthy, distant stretch of rocky corridor came into focus. A long line of heavily armored soldiers was marching along, blue-and-green battle standards raised. They dragged enormous wagons bearing trebuchets and catapults. They were clearly headed to war.

"An imperial battalion," Birgit explained. "Unless I'm mistaken, that's my sister, Gerwalta, leading them."

Esme's brow furrowed. She hadn't considered the possibility of Birgit having any friends, let alone having family. "Does your sister know you're—"

"And over there," Birgit said, spinning Esme by her shoulders, "is where they are headed."

Esme trained the spyglass on this new section of the canyon. She moved it left to right, unsure what Birgit had seen until . . .

There it was. The Onyx Maiden. It was an odd statue. It looked to be dressed like a warrior, but it sat with its back to the canyon wall. Not exactly a pose one would expect a warrior to take. Esme turned a dial on the spyglass, making the image of the Maiden fill the lens a little more.

"It moved!" she said, almost shouting. The statue was alive? Another fact the Nachtfrau had failed to mention.

"Troubling, isn't it?" Birgit said. "That statue sat in the center of Somber End for over ten years. Soothsayers warned that her awakening would bring great peril to the empire."

Esme knew little of soothsayers. The Collective had

always avoided her questions about divining the future. She was never sure if that was because they didn't think it was possible . . . or if they didn't know. One thing was sure: if foretelling the future was possible, it would take a Hierophant with enormous power.

"If you look closely at the army," Birgit continued, "you'll see they're following in the Maiden's footsteps." She pointed toward the soldiers, then drew a straight line through the air, ending at the Maiden. "They're coming to kill her."

"How do you know that?"

"Many attempts were made to destroy the Maiden in the past. All failed. If they're giving chase, they must have figured out a way to harm the statue. Gerwalta wouldn't be stupid enough to lead her finest troops to their deaths."

"But I need . . . what's in its chest." Esme couldn't bring herself to say she needed the Maiden's heart, especially now that she knew it was alive. That, of course, raised a whole new problem. How could she take the statue's heart without killing it?

"Then you should get going," Birgit said, her eyes fixed on the army, now close enough to be seen without the aid of the spyglass. "If you're going to warn them."

Esme frowned. "'Them'?"

Birgit nodded in the direction of the Maiden. "Look again."

Esme used the spyglass to focus on the statue once more. This time, she noticed a boy with rich brown skin standing on the Maiden's leg. He appeared to be talking to her.

"That," Birgit said, "is Prince Alphonsus. If he's with the Maiden, I'm afraid he's in as much danger as she is."

"Wait a minute. You said that *I* have to warn them. Not 'we.'"

Birgit looked toward Alphonsus as if she could see him without the spyglass. "I can't let him see me—the prince. Please don't ask why. It's . . . difficult to explain."

"I thought you were supposed to help me." Esme had hated every minute she'd spent with the huntress, but she hadn't bargained on an entire battalion bearing down on her. And she knew it might be of use if she had the sister of the oncoming general on her side.

"Oh, I'll still be helping. You just won't be seeing me as much. Now, please, we're running out of time. Warn the prince that the army is coming. From here, you can see the path that will take you there. Two left turns, two right. If you leave now and run, you should get to him before the soldiers arrive. But only just."

The girl squinted across the canyon toward the Maiden. "I don't need to run. I have . . . faster ways to get there."

Birgit nodded in understanding. "Two things before

you go . . ." She pulled a strip of tree bark from the satchel at her hip and handed it to Esme. "Your mother wanted you to have this. She said you'd need it to understand something important."

Esme inspected the bark. The outer side was rough and dappled brown and white. The smooth inner side bore four carved sigils Esme had never seen before. Below the symbols was a series of cants.

"What does she expect me to do with this?" Esme asked.

"Cast it, I should think."

Esme scrutinized the mysterious spell before placing it in her own sack. "What was the second thing?"

Birgit's face became solemn. Sad, even. "Please, whatever you do, don't tell the prince you've seen me. I can't explain why. But please. Don't mention me."

It seemed a strange request. But Esme nodded. She had no plans to see Birgit ever again. With any luck, she could quickly remove the Maiden's heart and be back to the Hexen Woods before sundown the following day. If Birgit wanted to disappear, that was her business.

Esme planted her feet. She didn't like this spell. The Balance was . . . unpleasant. But she didn't have a choice.

With her right hand, she quickly traced a constellation of whorls above her head. With her left, she sketched a separate set of symbols below her waist. She intoned the cant of each sigil in a deep voice that rattled around inside the bridge of her nose. As she did, the sigils began to glow with golden light in the air around her.

Shouting the final cant, Esme thrust her arms above her head. Like a swarm of gnats, the shimmering symbols descended on the Hierophant, bathing her in their light. Esme felt as if a thousand fishhooks had taken hold and were pulling her in every direction. The last thing she saw before she vanished in a flash was Birgit crawling over the edge of the mesa top to return to the canyon floor.

A foot-deep trench formed a jagged path
through the canyon. This happened only when the
creature was angry. Its churning became so fierce
that its movement tore a hole in the earth, leaving a
rocky wound in its wake. And at that moment, the
creature had never been angrier.

It was being taunted. It couldn't find the prey
it had been hunting. It couldn't find the one who
had spoken its name. Its fury growing, the creature
shattered boulders and shredded trees on its mission
of destruction. If it had to, it would tear down every
wall in the canyon. It would grind every mesa to
dust. It would drain every riverbed dry. As long as
the interlopers lived, nothing else would be able to.

It turned a corner and stopped.

It knew this place. This was a bad place. A very
bad place.

The creature felt invisible hands pressing in on it
everywhere. No matter how hard it battered against
the unseen, it could not move.

It looked up. There they were. Symbols as tall
as the canyon walls themselves, carved deep into

the rock. As the creature attempted to move past them, the symbols lit up with an eerie green glow and an unseen force pushed even harder, keeping the creature at bay.

It was not welcome here. It was not allowed.

The creature sulked. What had it done to deserve this punishment? Why couldn't it go wherever it wanted? It had seen these symbols in many places around the Hinterlands. Since this desolation was its home, it should be able to go anywhere. Yet the symbols told it: You are a prisoner.

Its prey lay beyond the symbols. The creature could sense it. There was life to be killed. And then deaths to be erased.

20

The Vision

LUCKILY FOR ALPHONSUS, THE CHILDREN WEREN'T SCARED for long. Within minutes, they seemed to think that holding his hand and running was a game. He wished he felt that way.

Sweat stung the prince's eyes as the sun's heat, bouncing off the canyon walls, threatened to bake them all alive. They ran until the screams of whatever had been bearing down on them had faded into nothing. This comforted Alphonsus. Whatever it was, it could be easily outrun. Or, at the very least, outsmarted.

He hoped.

When they could run no more, Alphonsus ducked

under the shade of an outcropping of rock. The two children snuggled up next to him, one on each side, and wrapped their arms around his waist. Alphonsus pulled out a crude flask, fashioned for him by the Maiden from the bones of an elk they'd encountered while still in the forest of Rheinvelt.

He offered the flask to the children, who drank gratefully.

"Can you take me where you live?" he asked. "We're almost out of water."

Alphonsus guessed they had to live close. He doubted they could survive in the Hinterlands this far from home. But the children didn't say anything. Instead, they nudged each other, each vying for the last drops of water.

"Leichleben," the boy had said. Alphonsus didn't know the word. It was probably in a language he didn't understand. He wouldn't get far with them if they didn't speak the same tongue.

But the girl had said "monster." *That* Alphonsus had understood.

"Listen," he said, gently taking away the empty flask so they would stop squabbling over it. "Where are your parents? Or family? How about your names? Can you tell me that?"

The children only giggled more and began rolling

around on the clay ground. Alphonsus drew a deep breath. If they couldn't lead him somewhere safe, their safety was up to him.

He closed his eyes and remembered the days he used to spend in the forest, training with Birgit. What had she taught him about survival? *Water.* He needed to find clean water above all else. *Shelter.* That came next. *Food.* They could go a couple days without it, if needed. But . . . then what? He was lost in the wilderness. When he'd run from Somber End with the Maiden, he hadn't really thought about where they'd go. Now he realized that he might have to live out the rest of his life among these unforgiving rocks.

Suddenly, the little boy squealed with fear, and both children scurried to hide behind Alphonsus as a shadow fell across them. A powerful rumbling shook the ground. Without thinking, the prince grabbed a rock and held it over his head, ready to smash whatever was coming their way.

The sun disappeared, blocked from view, as the Maiden came around the corner. She was dragging her flail behind her, accidentally digging furrows into the canyon floor.

Alphonsus exhaled sharply, partly from the fear draining from his body, partly from his happiness at seeing the statue. "It's okay," Alphonsus told the children. "You're safe."

But he hadn't needed to. As soon as the Maiden came into view, the children howled with delight and ran to her. The boy threw his arms around the Maiden's left ankle as far as they'd go while the girl climbed over the Maiden's toes, laughing all the while.

Alphonsus marched up to the Maiden and shook his finger. "You left me! I was worried."

The Maiden shook her finger right back and declared, "*Toe!*"

"They act like they know you. How is that possible?"

The Maiden reached down and gently prodded the little boy. He squirmed as if the statue's touch tickled. When the boy wouldn't move, the Maiden picked him up between two fingers and set him down in the prince's arms.

"They're like me," Alphonsus said, studying the boy's artificial leg. "Wherever they're from . . . that's where you're leading me."

The Maiden pointed over and over at the boy. Her finger was so large Alphonsus couldn't tell exactly what she was trying to indicate. But as he looked closer, he noticed the boy wore a silver triangle pendant bearing a small whorl.

"That looks like a Hierophant sigil," Alphonsus said. He'd learned about the mysterious Hierophants. He knew they commanded a strange alphabet that allowed them to wield magic. But that was all he knew . . . save the fact that there weren't supposed to be any Hierophants left in the land. "Are these Hierophant children?"

Alphonsus reached out to touch the pendant. As he did, he felt a jolt, much like the first time he'd touched the Maiden. The world went dark.

Suddenly, the prince felt as though he were lying on his back. He couldn't move. He could see that he was in a room. The walls were made of dirty beige muslin. Two long candles spread soft yellow light all around.

Screaming. He could hear screaming. A man and a woman. And something else . . .

The roar. The one that he and the two children had just run away from. It was louder than ever, threatening to drown out the terrified shrieks.

A flap in the canvas wall flung open. A man—his skin the same brown tone as the prince's—bolted in, a pale woman in his arms. Both wore masks that covered the top half of their faces. The man threw his mask aside as he helped the woman to her feet. She was dazed.

"You have to go," the man shouted. "Take Alphonsus!"

The great howl seemed to come from all around them.

Something—Alphonsus couldn't see what—tore the flap from the wall. The wooden pillars that held up the canvas buckled to some invisible force and flew through the air. The tent—the prince could see now that he was in a tent—collapsed around him. Chunks of wood and stone pierced the air, burying the man and woman. Alphonsus found himself screaming. But it didn't sound like him. It sounded like the cry of an infant.

Gasping, Alphonsus threw up his arms. Immediately, the vision vanished and the surrounding canyon returned. The prince staggered, breathing heavily. The small boy and his sister went to the prince's aid. They each held a hand, as if they understood what had just happened.

But how could they? Alphonsus didn't even understand.

"What was that?" he asked the Maiden. "Did you see it too?"

The Maiden pointed to the girl, then the boy, then to Alphonsus.

"Yes," the prince snapped, "I know. We're connected somehow. Stop pointing, stop disappearing, and help me! You led me out here into the wastelands, and I don't understand what's going on!"

As soon as he said this, Alphonsus was sorry he'd raised his voice. The Maiden didn't seem offended, though. She didn't even seem to know that he'd been angry. She just pointed once more to the girl, then to the boy, then to Alphonsus.

The prince sighed. "We're out of water. I'm trying to get them to take me to wherever they're from. Can you lead us there?"

The Maiden laid her open palm to the ground. The children stepped onto it, and the statue lifted them to her shoulder. She held out her hand to hoist Alphonsus to the other shoulder.

Crack! Something like a thunderbolt shook the ground, knocking Alphonsus down. His hair stood on end as the air nearby started to shimmer and swirl.

Crack! A girl appeared from nowhere. She had very pale skin and bright-red hair, and she glowed with a golden aura so bright that Alphonsus had to hide his eyes.

"Prince Alphonsus?" the girl asked. "My name is Esme Faust. I've come to help you."

21

The Rhyme and the Voice

Esme's eyes went immediately to the giant onyx statue. The Maiden was terrifying to behold. She towered over them all. Not quite tall enough to breach the top of the canyon walls, but big enough that Esme knew she'd be a formidable opponent when the time came to—

That's when she spotted the clock in the center of the Maiden's chest. *A clock?* That's what the Nachtfrau wanted? She wasn't sure it would even fit inside the infinitum box. But then the Nachtfrau hadn't really given the box to Esme to collect the heart in, had she? The bigger question was: How could she extract the clock? Surely, that meant killing the Maiden.

It's stone, she told herself. *Ordinary onyx. It's not really alive. The fact that it moves is only a trick. It's just an enchant-ment. Magic can't bring life. Can it?*

"You're . . . glowing."

Esme's attention snapped away from the Maiden, and she took her first real look at the boy standing before her. He was about her age, thin-framed, with big, innocent eyes. Since he was bare-chested, she noted that he, too, had a clock in his chest. But several of the numbers were missing. She stared at it so long that the boy nervously placed his hand over the clockface. Embarrassed, Esme looked away.

"What? Oh. Yes. That's . . . a side effect of the spell I used to get here. It will fade." Then she lowered her voice and grumbled, "Eventually."

The prince's eyes widened. "Spell? Are you a Hierophant? Have you come for the children?"

Esme shrugged. "What . . . children?"

Alphonsus stepped aside to reveal a young boy and girl. Like the prince, each had had a part of their body replaced with something unusual. They giggled and ran to Esme, throwing their arms around her in a big hug.

"Oh!" she said. "Er, no. I don't know them. I don't . . . I'm sorry, could you let go of me, please?"

Alphonsus smiled. "They're just very affectionate."

"I see that. I just . . . I haven't spent much time with children."

"But you're not much older than me."

"I know," Esme said, gently prying the children from around her waist. "Most of my life has been in the company of adults. I . . . relate better to them, I guess. Why did you ask if I'd come for them?"

Alphonsus put his arm around the boy and pointed at a pendant around the child's neck. He seemed afraid to touch it. "That's a Hierophant sigil, isn't it?"

Esme examined it. "Yes. It's a protective glyph. A very powerful one." Goose bumps tickled her skin, reacting to the unseen waves of magical energy pulsing from it. The Hierophant who had crafted the pendant was very skilled.

The little girl squealed and showed that she wore a similar pendant. So both the children were under protection. But by whom? And from what?

The prince's brow furrowed. "But . . . they're not with you? I thought they lived around here. With other Hierophants."

"The Hierophants are in the lands beyond the north sea. I'm the only one around here."

Esme coughed and placed her hand to her throat. She sounded hoarse. Getting sick made perfect sense. Everything else about this terrible trip had been a disaster. Why not add illness? But though her voice sounded weak, she felt fine.

"What did you mean?" Alphonsus asked. "When you said you've come to help."

"A battalion of soldiers is getting close. They're looking for you and . . . that." She nodded at the Maiden. The statue tilted its head as though it hadn't quite heard Esme. "I was sent to warn you."

The prince immediately looked suspicious. "Who sent you?"

Esme clenched her jaw to keep her rising impatience from bubbling over. "Does it matter? I'm a Hierophant, and I'm here to help. I can use the same spell I used to come here to take us someplace safe." *If you don't mind glowing for a while*, she added silently.

The prince ran to the statue. "This is exactly what we needed! A Hierophant. Between the two of you, we can force the Margrave to stand down."

The statue nodded once. "*Fire.*"

Esme grimaced, the Maiden's voice hurting her ears. "What are you talking about?" she asked.

"Hierophant Faust," Alphonsus said, suddenly very serious, "my empire is in grave danger. I need your help. A member of my mother's court is trying to overthrow our reign. It's his battalion that's on the way. But with your help, we can subdue him and see that justice is served. Please."

Esme frowned. She didn't care about the political battles

in Rheinvelt. She only wanted to free the Hierophants. The urge to transport them all away and figure out how to get the clock from the Maiden's chest burned in her fingertips.

But the prince seemed attached to the Maiden. Surely the fact that they both had clocks for hearts meant something. It wouldn't be easy to take the Maiden's. However, if the prince owed her a favor . . .

"Powerful as I am," she said reluctantly, "I can't take on an entire battalion."

"You won't have to," Alphonsus insisted. "The Maiden will help. And I don't want any violence. I'm hoping that, faced with the threat of her and you, the Margrave will surrender. We have to speak to Gerwalta. She must be leading the troops. She'll listen to me."

"And what if that doesn't work? What if we have to fight?"

The prince's shoulders slumped. "I . . . I don't know."

Esme felt annoyed. Mainly with herself. She was starting to take pity on the prince. "I . . . might know a way."

She reached into her satchel and pulled out the infinitum box. The prince stared at it warily.

"What is it?" he asked.

"It answers questions. You just . . . have to be careful of the answers."

The box wheezed and jolted in her hand. It had never done that before! Then, the box spoke.

> *"When nights pass as hours the same*
> *The end of time will start*
> *A sacrifice is all that saves*
> *The counterclockwise heart"*

Together, Alphonsus and Esme gasped.

"That rhyme!" Alphonsus said. "I know it. What does it—?"

"Shh!" Esme hissed. "Don't ask a question. We have to ask about defeating the battalion."

But she didn't do that. She stood there, hands trembling. The prince had recognized the strange rhyme. He hadn't seemed to notice that the box had spoken in *Esme's* voice.

She had noticed the box's voice—her father's voice—had changed each time she'd opened it. Getting higher and lighter. Now, there was no mistaking that it spoke as Esme. What was happening?

The Hierophant swallowed hard and asked, "How can we defeat the approaching battalion?"

The box shuddered again and exhaled a burst of foul-smelling air. *"Lure them into a dead-end valley, seal the exit, and trap them inside."*

Alphonsus, still confused by the rhyme, said, "I saw a valley like that when we were running. Not far from here. It has a narrow entrance. We can lead them there—"

"It gives two answers," Esme snapped, her voice weaker than ever. "Only one is the truth. Listen to both. Then we must decide which answer is right."

The box lurched so strongly that Esme almost dropped it. When it spoke again, Esme heard herself—confident and clear and very, very serious.

"You can't."

The rabbit was dying. It had been scurrying across the canyon floor when it crossed the Leichleben's path and was accidentally pierced by the shrapnel of an exploding stone. The poor animal bled from several holes. One of its rear legs had been torn clean off. Its breathing slowed.

A terrible low sound came from the very center of the swirling vortex that was the Leichleben. This was how it keened. This was how it mourned.

The creature hated death. Especially when it was an accident. It hated that the most. And all it wanted to do was help.

Helping was something it knew it could do.

A tendril of swirling air and sand snaked out from the core of the Leichleben. It plucked a purple reethee flower from the arm of a nearby cactus. With great force, the tendril turned and dove straight at the rabbit's chest. The sand and stone spun so quickly they acted like knives, slicing open a new hole. The Leichleben forced the flower into the rabbit's chest.

The animal jerked around as the petals wrapped

around its heart, squeezing it tightly until they became one. As the heart and reethee joined, the rabbit's wounds closed. The Leichleben's tendril scooped up a bent chunk of sandstone and fused it to the rabbit's hindquarters, fashioning a new leg. Then the creature moved away.

The rabbit quivered, unsure of what to make of what had just happened. It hopped forward cautiously, trying out its new stone leg. It blinked. It hopped. Then it scampered away, as if choosing to forget all of this.

The Leichleben felt satisfied. A wrong had been righted.

Now, to kill the interlopers.

Baiting the Trap

ALPHONSUS KEPT HIS HEAD DOWN AS THEY BACKTRACKED through the canyon, searching for the valley he'd seen. Every so often, his eyes darted to the sack around Esme's waist. The one where she kept the talking box.

The box that knew about the rhyme from his bassinet.

"You're upset about something," Esme said, sounding impatient. "What is it?"

The girl was very straightforward, if not the most sympathetic. The straightforwardness reminded Alphonsus of the empress. The lack of empathy did not.

"When you opened the box," he said, "it spoke a rhyme."

She sighed. "I don't know why it does that. I have no clue what it means. Have you heard it before?"

"Yes. Sort of."

"What does it mean?"

He shrugged. "I was hoping you could tell me."

"Well, I can't. It's just nonsense, isn't it? Nights and hours passing the same? It's ridiculous." She paused and fixed him with a quizzical look. "Did you know there are numbers missing from the clock in your chest?"

"This is it," Alphonsus said quickly, avoiding the question.

The opening in the canyon wall was cone-shaped and narrow. The soldiers would be forced to enter single file, slowing them down. The valley beyond was long and elliptical, with rocky terrain. Alphonsus imagined it might look like an eye from above.

Behind him, he could hear Esme grunt and groan as the children scrambled around her, trying to get her to pick them up. He stole a glance over his shoulder. Esme played a losing game, trying to extract her limbs from the children's enthusiastic (and tight) grips. She'd free one arm from the boy's grabbing hands only to find the girl wrapped around her leg. Alphonsus laughed to himself at the Hierophant's clear discomfort. She'd said she hadn't been around children much. More likely, he mused, it was that she'd never had the chance to be a child herself.

Nearby, the Maiden stood passively, as if awaiting the prince's orders.

When Esme finally freed herself, she joined Alphonsus. The Hierophant studied the entrance to the valley and nodded. "This should work. Good a place as any to set a trap."

Alphonsus looked her up and down. "Are you sure you're going to stop glowing?"

The Hierophant glared. "I'm *so sorry*, Your Highness, that my uncontrollable glowing bothers you."

"Well, you're definitely dimmer than before. But the sun's almost down. You're a beacon that will lead the battalion right to us."

"That's what we want, isn't it?"

Each time she spoke, she sounded more put out. For someone who claimed she'd been sent to help, she wasn't being very helpful.

The children had taken to tugging at the prince's arms, no longer seeking to be held but rather trying to get him to follow them. Alphonsus went down on one knee.

"Listen to me," he told them. "Bad things are going to happen here soon. It's very important that you leave and go back to your families. If everything works out here, I promise I'll come find you. I'm very interested to meet your people."

The children looked close to tears. They threw their arms around the prince's neck and squeezed. He hugged them back just as tightly. When they pulled away, the boy took the pendant from around his neck and offered it to Alphonsus. The prince took a step back.

Esme sighed. "I told you, it's not dangerous. It's a protective glyph. He wants you to be safe. It's . . . sweet, I guess."

Alphonsus shook his head. "No, thank you. I want *you* to be protected. Now, go. Find your family."

The children joined hands, turned as if to leave, then spun around and darted into the bottleneck valley, laughing all the way.

Alphonsus went to run after them, but Esme held him back. "If they want to stay, let them. We can protect them. If it becomes a battle, I'll turn them invisible so they won't be harmed."

"Thank you." The prince noticed her watching him. She looked both amused and curious. "What?"

"You're very kind to the children."

"Are Hierophants not kind to children?"

The girl flinched, as if the question had stung her. Or perhaps it was one she'd never considered. "My father was kind. The kindest man I knew. Others in our colony?

Well, they weren't exactly unkind. They tended to be strict."

Alphonsus shrugged. "My mother can be strict. She says it's because she loves me. I'm sure that's true of your family too."

The Hierophant averted her eyes. "Why were you afraid of the pendant?"

"I touched it before, and . . . something happened." He explained the strange vision he'd had, where he seemed to be lying on his back as a couple ran into the tent and were almost certainly killed when something terrible destroyed it.

Esme listened closely. "I've been told that some enchanted items—items imbued with a lot of power—can sometimes revive lost memories."

"That was a memory?" Alphonsus grappled with what that might mean. Who were the people who'd died? They'd spoken his name. Were they his birth parents?

"Maybe," Esme said. "I don't know for sure. Very few Hierophants can create enchanted items that strong. In fact, I can only think of one. The Nachtfrau."

Alphonsus scowled. "The evil sorceress who lives in the Hexen Woods? But she's a myth."

Esme only grunted in reply. Her gaze turned to the valley's conical entrance. "So, we lure the soldiers in through the opening. You and the Maiden are the bait that will bring them inside. You'll both be waiting at the other end. Once they're all past the entrance, I can detonate the entry walls. They'll collapse, and the battalion will be trapped."

"Then the Maiden can scale the canyon wall and take us with her."

"And then what?"

"We take the children home."

"Where is that?"

"I don't know. Somewhere in the Hinterlands. Maybe you can use your magic to find it."

Esme folded her arms. "If it isn't obvious to you by now"—she pointed to her brightly glowing face—"there are consequences whenever I use magic. And I can't always predict what those consequences will be. First, I'm supposed to blow up the valley entrance. Then I'm supposed to find the home of some . . . very strange children."

"Hey," Alphonsus snapped at her. "They're not strange."

"My point is: I'm not even from here. Not really. You're not *my* prince. And it seems that helping you stop an insurrection in the empire should be worth something. When this is all done, what will you do for me?"

At first, Alphonsus felt angry. He'd been taught to help others, especially when they were in trouble. It never would have occurred to him to barter his assistance for repayment. But it had become clear that Esme had had an . . . unusual upbringing. Things worked differently among the Hierophants. He didn't want to feel sorry for her . . . but he still did.

"Of course," the prince said. "Once we've stopped the insurrection, whatever is in my power to grant is yours. Just name your price."

He watched the girl closely. She peered over the prince's shoulder, in the direction of the Maiden. The statue stood silently, as if not even noticing the Hierophant's sudden interest.

Esme smiled. "We can talk about that later."

23

Emissary

GUNTRAM HAD LOST TRACK OF HOW MANY DAYS IT HAD been since the caravan of imperial soldiers had left Rheinvelt. It all blurred together: the days and nights, the identical, never-ending stone gorges of the Hinterlands. They marched and marched, only stopping for brief moments of rest. None in the battalion seemed to mind any of it. Many, in fact, seemed to enjoy the exhaustion, the mind-boiling heat, and the sleeping on rocks. How Guntram longed for his goose-feather bed back in the palace.

While Gerwalta and the empress led from the front of the ranks, Guntram had buried himself among the soldiers. He feared Prince Alphonsus might jump out from behind a rock at any moment and tell his mother about Guntram's treachery. If the Margrave was at the head of the line when this happened, his head would be liberated from his shoulders by the empress before he could even utter a protest. Huddled here among the troops, he at least would have a chance to run before word from the front of the line filtered back.

Gerwalta had proved as cunning a tracker as her sister, the royal huntress. Using ancient maps from the imperial library, she had deftly directed the troops through the maze of gullies and ravines in pursuit of the Maiden. The maps had even provided them with shortcuts, which allowed them to catch up much faster than they'd anticipated. Gerwalta now believed the Maiden was only a few hours away.

Guntram's heart beat so quickly he thought he might pass out. Soon, there would be a reckoning. He reminded himself over and over again to stay sharp and be ready.

That was when the sky caught fire.

Shortly before nightfall, a brilliant golden glow appeared on the horizon. It was so bright it blotted out the first stars of the evening. For an hour, the aura remained far away, stationary.

Then it began moving. Gerwalta ordered the troops to halt as everyone gaped at the radiance. It moved left. Then right. Then right again. It was making its way through the canyon. By the time dusk had fully come, there was no denying that the golden light was moving toward the battalion.

Guntram wove through the battalion to consult the empress and her captain at the front. Whispers slithered through the crowd. Guntram could see the warriors were all uneasy. No one wanted to guess what the approaching light meant.

Good. He wanted their imaginations to run wild. He wanted them to be afraid.

"Margrave," Gerwalta said, eyeing the approaching light warily. "Take the empress to the rear of the battalion. See to her protection."

But Sabine pulled away from Guntram's extended hand. "It could be the prince, bearing a torch. I'm staying here."

Gerwalta placed her hand on her sword hilt. "That's not torchlight." The captain of the guard was not one to easily show fear, but the quiver in her voice betrayed just how worried she was.

Guntram watched the light draw nearer, casting menacing shadows on the bend of the canyon wall before them. *It's her,* he thought. *She's taunting me.* He knew—*he just knew*—that the Maiden was challenging him. Daring him to come face her.

"Stand ready!" Gerwalta commanded.

All around Guntram, the soldiers went into action. Bow bearers drew arrows. The twilight filled with the sound of swords being drawn from scabbards. Only the empress didn't move. She stood staunchly, as if believing her love for the prince alone would protect her.

A girl rounded the corner just ahead. She held no torch, no lantern. *She* was the light. Her skin practically sparkled with golden radiance. She wore the clothes of a commoner, but her stern face had the resolve of someone with power.

"I come as an emissary of Prince Alphonsus," the girl called out to the battalion, her voice weak and cracking. "He asserts his authority as prince and orders you all to stand down now. He has asked for Gerwalta, captain of the guard, to come forward and parley. If you do, he promises the empress will be merciful."

Sabine stepped forward. "*I* am the empress, young lady. I will speak to my son and no emissary. Take me to him."

The girl looked taken aback. She clearly hadn't expected to find the empress among the soldiers. "How do I know you're telling the truth? I won't lead the prince's enemies to him."

Sabine offered a grudging smile. "You're very clever." She took a ring from her finger and handed it to the girl. "Show this to my son. He will verify my signet and know

I have come for him. When he's convinced, return and lead me to the prince."

The glowing girl looked unsure, then nodded. Without another word, she turned and walked away.

Guntram felt his chest tighten. If he had any hope of surviving this, it was now or never.

"Your Majesty," he said, making sure the soldiers could hear him. "I can't let you do this. It's too dangerous."

"I have nothing to fear from my son," Sabine said.

"I mean it's too dangerous for the empire. You know what the soothsayers foretold. The time of the Maiden's reckoning is upon us. She has claimed your son. You are letting your love for him blind you to the idea that he is lost. He belongs to her now. You are putting the entire empire at risk."

Sabine looked genuinely surprised, as if she had no idea that Guntram would ever be brave enough to challenge her. "Be careful, Margrave."

But Guntram was just getting started. "When you and the imperatrix first heard of the Maiden's appearance, you stayed in your palace and sent others to investigate. You've never even seen her in person. You don't know her. I do. I stared into her cold, lifeless eyes every day for ten years. I know the way she thinks. She is pure evil. If you bring the prince back into the fold without destroying her, you are bringing someone touched by her evil to the royal bosom. We could all be killed."

Behind him, Guntram could hear the soldiers shuffling uncomfortably. He half expected to feel the tip of a sword press against the small of his back. When none did, it emboldened him.

The empress drew a long, deep breath. "Captain," she said, "arrest the Margrave. When we retrieve the prince and return to the palace, the Margrave will be tried for treason."

Before Gerwalta could draw her sword, Guntram leapt onto a rock and addressed the battalion. "Your empress has been lying to you! The Maiden didn't just mark Prince Alphonsus with the clock in his chest. He's had it his entire life! The empress welcomed the Maiden's tool into the royal palace, knowing full well about the clock in his chest. She has harbored an enemy of the realm for ten years and lied to you about it the whole time! Tell them, Empress. Tell them the truth for once."

A cold murmur snaked its way up from among the soldiers' ranks. "Who is the prince really?" one inquired. "How could you hide that from your subjects?" another asked. But the loudest of the protests demanded to know: "Why?"

Sabine maintained her steely resolve and stared down the discontent. "How long the prince has had the clock isn't important. He is my son. *Your* sovereign. You've known him all your lives, and you know him to be a kind and gentle—"

"We believe the guardian!" someone toward the back shouted.

"Guntram knows the Maiden best!"

"Your son is a filthy traitor!"

"The Maiden must die!"

More and more voices added to the tumult as the soldiers closed in, forming a circle around the empress and Gerwalta. The captain and Sabine, both highly trained warriors, stood back-to-back, instinctively assuming a defensive position.

Guntram came down from the rock. "It seems I was wrong. It's not just the prince who has been bewitched by the Maiden. Clearly, the captain and our empress are also under her thrall. Bind them."

Sabine and Gerwalta moved as one. They drew their swords in a single synchronized gesture. The cool air seemed to thrum around everyone. Gerwalta met her soldiers' eyes, almost daring them to strike first. The empress, Guntram noted, never took her eyes off him. He knew there and then that if she made it to him, he'd never leave the Hinterlands alive.

In a moment lost to frenzy and history, someone moved first. A soldier? The captain? The empress? It's unknown. But, in an instant, the canyon walls hummed with the ricocheted clamor of steel on steel. Gerwalta's skill with a sword was known throughout the empire. She demonstrated her prowess over and over, fending off soldiers she herself had trained. Spinning and thrusting, she disarmed them rather than dispatching them. Sabine fought with less restraint, inflicting grievous wounds on anyone with the temerity to stand between her and the Margrave.

Both women put up a vicious fight, but in the end, they were no match for the entirety of the battalion. Now bound together with a combination of ropes and chains, neither posed a threat anymore.

Otto strode to Guntram's side, his hardened face and tight lips the very model of loyalty to the Margrave. "Let's leave them here," he suggested.

Guntram weighed his options. The wedding was off now—that much was sure. Once the Maiden was destroyed, he could return triumphantly to Rheinvelt with the battalion and they'd spread the word about how Guntram was victorious. It would be difficult for Sabine to execute someone that everyone knew was a hero.

Still, surely there were some here, even now, who might be nervous about the idea of challenging the empress. It would only take one to report back to the lords and ladies of the palace about what had happened here.

Clearly, the empress and captain needed to die. But it would be better if they died in battle.

"No," Guntram said, "bring them with us. Perhaps if they witness us destroying their onyx mistress, it will break the statue's hold on them. We might still save both the empress and the prince from the Maiden."

Sabine spit right into Guntram's eye. He flinched. "I am no pawn of the Maiden, Margrave. And when the statue is destroyed, you will see just how in control I am of my own actions. I will kill you with my bare hands if any harm comes to the prince."

Guntram wiped his face clean, drew his onyx-laden sword, and raised it to the evening sky. He turned to face the army. *His* army.

"Destroy the Maiden and any who stand in our way!"

24

Bound

BACK IN THE VALLEY, ESME WATCHED ALPHONSUS TURN
the ring over and over again in the palm of his hand.
"And you're sure it was my mother? The empress? What
did she look like?"

The Hierophant clenched her jaw. "Dark skin . . .
sturdy . . . grumpy . . . Is the ring hers?"

"Yes, definitely. But . . . I suppose someone could have
stolen it from her."

They stood at the far end of the eye-shaped valley.
Nearby, the two children scaled the Onyx Maiden, who
seemed to enjoy the attention.

"Well, Your Highness, you need to decide." Esme
hoped it was the empress. She hoped the empress grabbed

the prince and then sent her soldiers to deal with the Maiden. She'd been eyeing the statue for a while now. She wasn't sure she knew a spell powerful enough to take the Maiden down in one blow. And she didn't exactly want to give the statue a chance to strike back. It would be easier if the battalion took her—*it*—down.

Alphonsus nodded and put the ring in his pocket. "If she's there, she'll listen to me. I can tell her about the Margrave. I can fix all this."

"Yes, that's what you should do. Go fix this. I'll wait here . . . with the Maiden."

"Watch after the children," the prince said, then he started the long walk across the narrow valley.

As Alphonsus grew distant, Esme reviewed her plan in her head. When the battalion arrived, they would engage the Maiden. Esme would cast a spell and render herself invisible. Then she'd wait in the shadows until the soldiers had destroyed the statue. After they left, Esme could sift through the rubble, retrieve the clock from the Maiden's chest, and return with it to the Nachtfrau. It was perfect.

Except.

"You two!" she snapped over to the children. "You should leave. It's going to be very dangerous here. Go home. Go . . . wherever. Just go." They kept playing on the statue.

The Maiden looked at Esme. Her stony features

moved slightly, changing to what Esme could only imagine resembled a facial shrug.

Esme scoffed and sat down on the rocky valley floor. *Let them stay.* She wasn't responsible for them.

As she leaned back, she felt a sharp pain in her side. The piece of bark given to her by Birgit was sticking out of her sack. She'd forgotten about it. Holding the bark to her small lantern, Esme peered at the sigils scrawled across it. The nature of this spell remained a mystery, the sigils unknown. She had always believed that the Hierophant Collective had given her the sum of their knowledge, taught her every cant and every sigil they knew.

So why did she not know these?

What does the Nachtfrau expect me to do with this? Esme wondered.

From some corner of her mind, she imagined Birgit Freund answering in her most patronizing tone. *Cast it, I should think.*

"Let's get this over with," she muttered. She practiced drawing the sigil in the air a few times before finally completing the pattern and whispering the cant.

Her vision clouded over. Everything around her disappeared into a blur of dark ocher and gray. Then, the hazy colors became shapes again. When at last she could see, she was no longer in the valley. She was standing deep in a forest at dusk. A light drizzle mixed with a thin mist that rose off the ground, leaving every tree and rock glistening.

She knew she wasn't actually there. She couldn't smell the pine or feel the light rain. But everything she could see was crystal clear.

"Ah! Is that you? Are you there?"

She heard the Nachtfrau's voice, tinny and hollow-sounding, as though she were speaking into a glass jar.

"Where are you?" Esme asked.

"The Hexen Woods, of course. I told you I can't leave."

Esme tried turning her head, but what she saw remained the same: a fixed view of a smattering of wet bushes. "I'm seeing through your eyes."

She heard the Nachtfrau chuckle. "As a child, my brothers would torment me by hiding somewhere on our father's land. I'd use this spell to find them. It was easy to figure out where they were from what each was seeing. You may find your sense of smell isn't quite as sharp for a while after we sever the connection, though. That's the Balance, I'm afraid."

"What do you want?" Esme asked, impatience coloring her voice. "Why did you give me this spell?" Again, she noticed how soft her voice had become. She could barely whisper.

"So we could talk. And before you think about using it to talk to the Collective, you should know it only creates a connection between two people of like blood. If I wanted to, I could cast it and see through *your* eyes."

But you've already done that, haven't you? Esme thought. That must be how her mother had known how much the Collective had taught her. It's how she'd known what Esme's true mission was in the first place. The Nachtfrau had been spying on her all her life. Through Esme's own eyes.

"Tell me," the Nachtfrau continued, "have you found the Maiden yet?"

"Yes. I'll have what you need very soon."

"Excellent! Will you be back by morning? Should I have breakfast ready?"

"You've been here before," Esme said. "In the Hinterlands. I saw Hierophant sigils carved into the canyon walls. I've never seen anything like them. You must have carved them, or the Collective would have taught me what they mean."

Her mother looked down at the ground, filling Esme's vision with wet grass. "Oh, the Collective knows what those symbols mean. But, yes, I carved them."

"What do they do?"

"They're binding sigils. They've been keeping something from getting out of the Hinterlands."

The jagged and rough terrain in the valley cut into his bare feet with each step. He remembered what he'd learned from Birgit about fighting. It would be hard for the soldiers to negotiate the rocky earth in their armored boots. It would slow them down when they tried to cross the valley.

If, Alphonsus reminded himself. *If they attack. Which they won't do if Mother is with them.*

He exited the valley and reentered the canyon maze. He could just make out a wall of light ahead and the outline of the battalion. The prince came to a stop as a single figure broke away from the rest of the soldiers and advanced. It was far too tall to be his mother.

With only moonlight between them, Guntram and Alphonsus stood face-to-face.

"Your Highness," the Margrave said with a sneer. "You're looking well."

Alphonsus felt the contents of his stomach churn. The last time he'd seen Guntram, the royal advisor had tried to kill him. Alphonsus made sure to keep his distance. He could still feel the Margrave's powerful fingers around his throat.

Run, a voice inside him said. *That's all you know how to do.*

"Where is my mother?" he asked. He tried to sound stern, but his voice squeaked.

"Tell me something," the Margrave said. "What did you say to her? How did you convince her that you were worth . . . anything?"

"What?"

"The Maiden. I know you said something to her. Lies. Lies that made her think you were worthy. That made her mark you as her equal." Guntram's voice had grown lower, more like a growl. His eyes never left the clock in the prince's chest.

"I told her exactly what *you* told me to tell her," Alphonsus shot back. "It's not my fault—"

"Liar!"

For a moment, Alphonsus thought the Margrave was going to strike him. He lifted an arm, prepared to deflect an incoming blow. But Guntram made no move. For the first time, his crazed gaze lifted from the clock and he stared the prince right in the eyes.

"Go," Guntram commanded in a breathy whisper. "Go and tell her that I'm coming. Tell her that she'll regret passing me over. And when I'm finished with her . . . you're next."

The Margrave turned on his heel and marched quickly back toward the battalion, shouting, "Prepare to attack!"

Esme's thoughts galloped. *Binding sigils?* The Collective had never even mentioned that such sigils existed.

"Meant to keep *what* here?" she asked. "Me?"

"Goodness, no, cub. Why would I want to trap you there?"

"Because you're evil."

The Nachtfrau sighed so fully that the noise filled Esme's head, momentarily blocking out other sounds. "Esme, your father died before he could teach you about things more powerful than magic. No sigil, no cant, can work the wonders that simple kindness can. You've no reason to believe me, but I hope that's something you understand someday—"

Esme waved her fingers, canceling the spell. Her vision blurred again, and then she could once more see into the valley. She wasn't about to listen to the Nachtfrau talk about her father.

The binding sigils. The secret city. The list of knowledge the Collective had kept from her was growing. The question wriggled inside her. *Why?*

There was, she knew, a way to learn. Slowly, she pulled the infinitum box from her pouch. She opened it and listened to her own voice—full and clear—recite the rhyme. Then she whispered, "Why did the Collective—?"

Even before the war trumpet's cry ricocheted off the sandstone valley walls, the crunch of armored boots marching heralded the battalion's arrival. Esme spun toward the valley's entrance, where she could just make out the silhouettes of the soldiers, lit by their own torches. And racing toward her at top speed was Alphonsus. She knew instantly that the prince's efforts to broker peace with the woman who'd claimed to be his mother had failed.

"They're here!" he shouted to her. "Get ready to seal the entrance!"

Esme snapped the box shut and traced the sigil that would make her invisible. But when she tried to speak the cant, nothing came from her mouth. She tried over and over, her hands flailing as she made the correct gestures. But she couldn't speak.

She stared at the infinitum box. Of course she couldn't speak. The voice she used for magic was now trapped inside the box. That was why it now sounded like her. It had been stealing her voice bit by bit, ever since she'd first opened it.

In moments, the prince was at her side. He studied her face. "What's wrong?"

"I can't speak the cants," she squawked in a hoarse rasp. "I can't use magic!"

25

War Cry

"But you need to cast the spell," Alphonsus said. "The box said that was the way to defeat the soldiers."

Esme glared at him. "I *know* that. I've tried." To prove it, she again traced a sigil over her head and when she tried to speak, nothing came out. "The box did this to me. It took the voice I use for magic."

The Maiden let loose a terrifying war cry. She'd spotted the battalion at the valley's entrance.

"Come here," Alphonsus said to the children. They didn't need to be told twice. As much as they'd grown attached to the statue, she had scared them. They scrambled off the Maiden, the girl running to Alphonsus for comfort while the boy ran to Esme.

"We need to take cover," Alphonsus said. "The Maiden will protect us." As if she'd heard him, the statue moved forward to meet their approaching foes.

Esme fumbled. With one hand, she tried to pry the small boy off of her. With the other, she pointed frantically at the battalion. "What about your mother? Why isn't she stopping this?"

"I . . . I don't think she's with them. No, she can't be. She'd never allow this."

Another blast sounded from the battalion's trumpets. With a united shout, the soldiers began their charge. Alphonsus watched as the Maiden planted herself halfway across the valley, her flail at the ready.

The air whizzed with the sound of arrows. The prince expected them to break harmlessly on the Maiden's onyx armor, as all other weapons in the past had done. Instead, these arrows sank deep into her, causing the statue to cry out in confusion.

By now, most of the battalion had swarmed around the Maiden's feet. They hacked at her with battle-axes and swords. The statue staggered and grunted as if surprised.

"Something's wrong," Alphonsus muttered. The Maiden was unbreakable, but the soldiers were clearly harming her.

A trebuchet at the rear sent a massive stone flying through the air. The light from Esme's glowing skin—growing fainter by the minute—was just enough to cast a sparkle on the chunks of onyx embedded in the missile. Suddenly, Alphonsus knew what was happening.

At the last moment, the Maiden ducked and the trebuchet's stone exploded in the valley wall just over Esme and Alphonsus. They scrambled to avoid the falling debris, leaping in opposite directions.

The Maiden let loose another roar. *"Foot!"* she declared, and reared back her leg and kicked. Two dozen soldiers flew through the air.

"Toe!" The Maiden kicked out again, this time striking out with the front of her foot. More soldiers fell.

This could still work, Alphonsus thought. *She might win.*

The little boy cried out. His sister took the boy's hand. Together, they stared up at the rim of the canyon wall at the other end of the valley.

"Leichleben!" the girl shouted.

Alphonsus followed her gaze. Something had appeared behind the soldiers, poised on the top of the canyon wall. Moonlight seemed to avoid this thing. Squinting, Alphonsus could see that it was constantly moving. A living storm of shadows that whirled around like a tornado but remained in one place. It hovered. It imposed.

It roared.

The sound it made filled the valley, rivaling the Maiden's own screech. A single long tendril of black wind swooped down into the bottleneck, engulfing a trebuchet and spitting it out in a flurry of splinters.

The battalion's fierce bellowing turned to screams of terror. Some continued to fight the Maiden. Others started a strategic retreat, running back through the entrance to the valley while they still could.

Esme, eyes wide, backed away. "I've heard that noise before. That thing was hunting me. What is it?"

"I don't know," the prince confessed. He turned to the children. "What do you mean, 'Leich—'?"

But the girl and boy were gone.

The soldiers that hadn't retreated pushed a second trebuchet into the valley and fired another boulder at the Maiden. This one hit her elbow, shattering it. The statue's severed forearm and hand fell to the ground and broke like glass into a thousand shards. The Maiden howled in pain.

"No!" Alphonsus cried.

"You can't do anything." Esme held him by the shoulders.

The Maiden drew back her right arm and swung her flail. Dozens of soldiers fell to the ground as the deadly spikes split the air. The Maiden growled. As if in response, on the other side of the valley, the shadowstorm creature began to descend the canyon wall.

Alphonsus kept struggling, but Esme was strong. She pulled him until their backs were against the wall. The prince couldn't take his eyes off the creature. What if it attacked the Maiden too?

His focus broke when Esme slapped his shoulder. "We need to go somewhere safe," she said. "Look." She nodded to a crevasse in the canyon wall. Alphonsus hesitated, torn between warning the statue and staying safe.

Suddenly, the Maiden's ferocity increased. She spun the flail over her head, faster and faster, until each strop became a blur. She started striking out blindly, the flail's onyx spikes hitting soldiers and earth and anything else in their way.

Alphonsus and Esme ducked as the spikes passed over their heads and punctured holes in the canyon wall.

"Stay if you want," Esme said, scurrying through the crack in the wall.

Alphonsus waited only a moment before he followed her. Esme's dim glow lit the interior, revealing a long, winding cave. The prince knelt down, scooped something shiny up off the cave floor, and showed it to

Esme. It was a pendant like the ones the children were wearing.

"They came in here," Alphonsus said.

"Where did they get these pendants?"

"I don't know."

Esme blinked quickly, like she was thinking a hundred thoughts at once. "I think I do. Somewhere in the Hinterlands is a . . . secret city. It belonged to the Hierophants. We need to find it."

"Why?"

"You wanted my magic to help you? Well, I can't do anything unless I can speak the cants. I might find something in that city that will force the box to give me my voice back. And you want to find the children, right? If they got these pendants from that city, they might be on the way back there."

Alphonsus closed his eyes. Outside, the battle raged on. He wanted to help the Maiden. At the same time, he knew he couldn't. He was too afraid. And that made him ashamed.

But there was also the matter of his clock and the disappearing numbers. If it was as he believed, he would die when the last number vanished. Finding the children—and maybe finding where he'd come from—could help him reverse that. He hoped.

Going with Esme gave him one more chance to save the empire. If the young Hierophant could do as she promised, he might still become the prince his people deserved.

Alphonsus opened his eyes. "Let's go find your secret city."

It stared at the statue. The statue stared back.

The fighting was over. Most of the soldiers had run from the valley. Bodies lay at the statue's feet. The creature keened softly for them. It hadn't caused the deaths. That made it both happy and sad.

The statue stared down at the stump that used to be its left arm. The creature moved across the valley floor. It expanded until it could completely engulf the trebuchet. It removed the weapon's throwing arm, went to the statue, and swiftly attached it to what remained of the statue's broken appendage.

The statue flung the new attachment about, trying out its new arm, now seamlessly part of its body, as if it had always been there. As one, the statue and the creature looked down at the dead. They exchanged unheard words, and the statue walked backward, hiding itself in the shadows.

The creature wandered among the dead. Just as it could hear its name whispered for miles, the Leichleben could also hear even the tiniest bit of life. Somewhere, among the bodies, it could hear breathing. Faint, weak breaths. The creature moved from body to body until it found the noise.

A man, his face slashed and bleeding, lay on the ground, a gaping wound in his chest. He shuddered, fighting to cling to the few moments he had remaining. The Leichleben took pity on him. It reached down and plucked a chunk of onyx from a pile that had once been the statue's arm. The black wind tendril raised the onyx high in the air and then plunged it down into the man's chest.

The man shook and screamed as the enchanted onyx joined with his flesh. The stone pulled at arteries and capillaries and blood, forcing the man's insides to bow to their will. When the Leichleben pulled its tendril out, the man sat up with a gasp. He touched his chest to find his wound healed. And he laughed. He laughed and laughed.

The Leichleben knew little of the world and the people who inhabited it. Still, it somehow knew what this man felt. The Leichleben knew these feelings well: fury, desire for revenge, an urge to destroy. The man crawled around on the valley floor, grasping in the dark until his hands found a large sword. He started muttering to himself, quietly but growing louder. The same words, over and over:

"Kill the prince."

The man ran away.

The creature immediately regretted saving him. This always happened. It saved things, and then they left. It decided to kill the man for not showing gratitude. But before it could move in pursuit, it heard that sound again. More feeble breathing. Not everyone here was as dead as they appeared.

The Leichleben searched until it found the second person on the cusp of death. A woman this time. She wore a gold-and-chrome breastplate. She, too, bore a wound in her chest, no doubt caused by the statue's flail.

This time, the creature found a battle-axe, broke off a chunk of its blade, and thrust the sharp steel into the woman's chest. Like the man before her, she could feel the cool metal take over the role of her heart and restore her to life.

The woman stood, dazed but recovering. She stared up at the Leichleben, her eyes wide with wonder.

"Thank you," she said.

The Leichleben no longer wanted to kill the man who'd run away. It wanted to stay here in this moment and bask in the woman's thanks. No one had ever said this before.

The creature let loose a terrible howl. A moment later, the statue stepped from its hiding place and reached out to the woman. Her body jolted and her eyes squeezed shut, as if the statue's touch had changed her. When her eyes opened again, they were filled with new wisdom and understanding.

The woman touched her recently healed chest, looked up at the statue, and said, "Save my son."

PART THREE

26

Lost

SOMEWHERE, IN THE NORTH LANDS, THE HIEROPHANTS were dying. A brutal winter storm that had lasted almost ten years raged on and on. Most guessed that everyone would be dead by year's end. Their single hope for survival—Esme Faust—sat in a damp, dark cave in the Hinterlands outside Rheinvelt. She hadn't spared a thought for her home in several days.

If her companion, Prince Alphonsus, was to be believed, they'd been lost in the underground warrens of the Hinterland canyon walls for almost four full days now. How he knew this, she wasn't quite sure. They hadn't seen daylight in all that time. Her skin had finally stopped glowing, and they'd had only the light of her lantern to guide them. But even that was down to its last few drops of oil. Soon, they'd be in total darkness.

During their wanderings, Esme might have worried about the Hierophants. She might have regretted making a bargain with the Nachtfrau to end the curse in exchange for the Maiden's heart. She might have bemoaned the numerous obstacles that had slowed her on her mission. Instead, her thoughts focused on Birgit Freund's annoying question: *Who are you without your magic?*

Esme had just spent the past four days learning. And all signs suggested she was nothing without magic.

The entire time she and the prince had been lost, Alphonsus had tried to keep a conversation going. He told Esme all about Rheinvelt; his late mother, the imperatrix; his living mother, the empress. Oh, how he talked about the empress. She was wise! She was just! She was kind! He asked the young Hierophant question after question about herself. But she would rarely summon more than a handful of words in response.

Without magic, she couldn't even carry on a polite conversation.

As the days wore on, she felt worse and worse. She realized that when this was all done and she returned to her people, she'd be going back to what she'd always known. More magical training. More spell casting. More scorn from Hierophants outside the Collective. She wasn't sure that was what she wanted anymore.

She and the prince had stopped for a short break. They both leaned against the rocky wall of a narrow passage. Each slowly munched on the last of the food they'd pooled together. The water would be gone soon, and as far as either knew, they were no closer to finding the way out. They would die in these caves.

"Why are you even helping me?" she asked.

Alphonsus wiped berries from his lips with the back of his hand. "We're helping each other."

"You needed me to use magic to stop insurrection in your empire. I'm useless now. I can't cast a single spell. You should've just left me behind."

The prince seemed confused. "I don't value people for their ability to perform magic."

"It's the only way I know how to value people," Esme whispered.

"Do you think less of me because I don't know how to draw sigils or speak cants?"

"Honestly? Yes."

The prince chewed more slowly. He looked as if she'd started speaking another language.

"You're not useless," Alphonsus finally said. "You're . . . you were good with the children. They liked you."

The prince's tireless optimism drained Esme of her

patience. "I appreciate you trying to make me feel better, Your Highness—"

"Call me Alphonsus."

Esme sighed. "I wish they were here so you could really see how not good I am with them."

They never had found the two strange children. In fact, they'd given up their search when they realized how lost they themselves were. Getting out alive had become more important. They couldn't help anyone if they were stuck in here.

"You're so interesting, Esme." When the prince spoke, he sounded excited at this idea. As if he *enjoyed* meeting "interesting" people. "Interesting" people tended to make Esme uncomfortable.

"Is that good or bad?"

"Good. Interesting people make me think."

"How do I make you think?"

"When you meet someone, you immediately assess their value. Do they use magic? Can they help you?"

Esme waved this away. "Everyone does that."

"Not everyone."

"Oh, really? You value me because you think I can rescue your empire."

"If you never get your magic back, I'll still value you."

The young Hierophant shifted. This "interesting" prince was making her uncomfortable. "Why?"

He laughed. "Because you make me think! What's more valuable than that?"

Esme turned away. The Collective had never encouraged her to think. To be strategic, yes. To learn the complex pronunciation of cants, certainly. But . . . *think*? If anything, thinking had been discouraged. She'd been taught obedience. To react *without* thinking. That there was no problem magic couldn't solve.

The Collective had never taught her how to solve problems without magic. It seemed that was a lesson the Nachtfrau and her infinitum box were determined for Esme to learn.

"Can that magic box help us?" Alphonsus nodded toward the sack where Esme kept the infinitum box.

"The 'magic box' is why we're in this mess," she answered, scowling. "It's been stealing my voice, bit by bit."

"What does that mean? You said it stole the voice you use for magic. How can you have two different voices?"

Esme searched for a way to sum up what had taken an entire year of her training in magic. "When we speak the cants, we do it in tone. It's a bit more than speaking. We find the exact pitch. In stealing my voice, it's taken all the tones I need for cants. And I don't think it's finished. I can barely talk now. Pretty soon, the box will have my whole voice."

The prince slowly lowered himself into a crouch, his eyes never leaving where he thought the box was. "Why . . . why did it speak that rhyme?"

"I told you. I don't know. It always does that. I have no idea what it means."

Alphonsus leaned forward into the dying lantern's meager light. He pointed to the clock in his chest. "Look closely."

Esme studied it. She noticed first that there were eight numbers missing total. She was convinced there had been more numbers when she'd first met the prince. But then she noticed the second hand. "It's moving backward."

"Counterclockwise," the prince corrected. He explained how he was found in the imperial palace walls in a bassinet with that rhyme inscribed on the bonnet. Then he traced the edge of the clock, the tip of his finger running over the blank spots where numbers should have been. "One number has vanished every day since I left the palace."

So that's how he'd known how long they'd been lost in the warrens. Esme touched the clock. If what he was saying was true, there were only four days left until . . . what? She remembered the rhyme. "'A sacrifice is all that saves—'"

"'The counterclockwise heart,'" they finished together.

As Alphonsus had already done quite some time ago, Esme pieced together the connection between the rhyme and the prince's clock, and her eyes widened in shock. "Alphonsus, are you dy—?"

"We're going to get out of here," the prince announced, jumping to his feet. "We don't have magic. We can't trust the box. We're out of food. *Almost* out of water . . ."

"I hope you're not trying to make me feel better."

"We know what we *don't* have. So what *do* we have?"

They both emptied their pouches, searching for something—*anything*—that might help them find their way out. They placed everything in a small pile. They had shiny stones Alphonsus had been collecting along the way. They had the maps the Collective had given Esme to find her way to the Hexen Woods.

Alphonsus picked his mother's ring out from the pile. The silver setting curled around a blue-green gem in the shape of an arrow. "Mother loved this ring."

Esme noticed he said "loved," as if he believed the empress was no more. She admired the ring. "I'm sure she's okay. When we find her, you can give—" She paused. She squinted in the light. "Can I see that?"

She took the ring and held it closer to the lantern. "This is a starstone."

"Yes," Alphonsus said. "They're very rare."

Esme shook her head. "You don't understand. Starstones react to daylight. If they're in the dark and daylight is near, they start to sparkle . . ."

She took off down the passage, holding the ring out in front of her. When she got to a three-way fork, she held the ring out in each direction. The silver molding of the ring vibrated in her hand as the starstone faced the right-hand passage. Ever so softly, the gem started to twinkle with dots of faint purple light.

Alphonsus jogged up behind Esme, his arms cradling the pile of their belongings that the Hierophant had left behind. He smiled when he saw the ring. "Is it magic?"

"No," Esme said. "It's just an ordinary rock that reacts to the presence of sunlight." It was still dark in the caves. But this ring would lead them outside.

They quickly repacked their belongings and headed down the right passageway, the ring lighting their way with a pale luminescence.

"See?" Alphonsus said. "I said you weren't useless."

But she didn't hear him. At that precise moment, a familiar voice in her head whispered, *Very clever, cub.*

Esme and Alphonsus continued to weave their way through the tunnels. The starstone grew brighter and brighter with each step. Soon, they could hear the sound of rushing air. The lantern ran out of oil, but dim light, reflected from an exit just ahead, continued to guide them forward. For the first time in days, they felt real hope.

That was when they heard the screams.

Esme knew those voices: it was the two strange children they'd failed to find. Together, she and Alphonsus ran through the final shaft toward the exit.

They emerged from a jagged crack in the wall to find themselves back in the Hinterlands desert. A small oasis—a pond, some trees and bushes—surrounded them. Esme scanned the area until she spotted the children on the other side of the clearing.

The little girl held her brother protectively behind a large bush. On either side, hulking monsters approached the children, claws extended. Esme recognized them. These were the same beasts that had attacked her when she first arrived in the Hinterlands. Viewing them in the daylight, she now saw that the humanlike creatures were covered in wiry, dirty white fur. Wide scars covered the juncture of each appendage. Great fangs protruded from their mouths, just below three withered eyes. They didn't look natural in any way.

Esme didn't even stop to think. She reached down, grabbed the first rock she could find, and hurled it. The closest beast squawked in pain as the rock bounced off its skull, opening a small wound. The creatures—three in all—turned their attention from the small children and growled at Esme and the prince.

Alphonsus stepped back, fear in his eyes. "You made it mad."

"That's okay," Esme said. "*I'm* mad. In fact, I've decided that's who I am without magic. *I'm mad.*"

Esme turned into a machine. Like a windmill, her arms swooped down, snatched up rocks, and twisted to catapult them at the beasts. Alphonsus, looking ill, followed her lead. Most of the time they missed. The creatures seemed confused to watch the stones fly past. But as Esme and Alphonsus grew tired, the beasts reared up and charged.

"Get. Back."

The voice that boomed out sounded more like a bear's growl than anything else. Whoever had spoken, the advancing creatures recognized immediately. The beasts whirled around. Standing just behind them, Esme saw a great hulk of a man wearing furry animal pelts. A mask made of cracked clay covered his face from the nose up, and a great black beard spilled down half his chest. His right arm was missing from the elbow down. In place of a forearm and hand, the man had a wooden device that ended in a crossbow. The weapon was loaded with a long silver-tipped arrow and it was pointed directly at the creatures.

"You know me," the man said. "And you know what I can do."

The hairy creatures hissed at one another, then skulked off down the canyon, away from the crossbow-wielding man. The brother and sister leapt out from behind the bush, ran to the man, and embraced him. Esme and Alphonsus just stared at each other, unsure what to make of their rescuer.

The small girl climbed up the man's chest, using his beard as a ladder, perched herself on his shoulder, and whispered in his ear. The man looked over, his eyes resting on Alphonsus. More specifically, on the prince's clock. He pushed his half mask up to his forehead, revealing a pair of striking green eyes.

"You're right," the man bellowed with a laugh. He tussled the young girl's hair. "He is most definitely one of us."

27

The Monster and
the Maiden

ALPHONSUS AND ESME FOLLOWED THEIR RESCUER—THE man, whose name was Aharon—past the oasis and back into the depths of the Hinterlands' endless canyons. Alphonsus gratefully accepted a cloth bandana from the young boy and wrapped it around his forehead. The caves had been considerably cooler than outside. Now, with the sun bearing down, the prince found himself drained by the merciless heat.

"Geist isn't far," Aharon said. He was far friendlier than his gruff tone suggested. "You're lucky those two"—he pointed to the two children, who had just wrapped themselves around Esme—"came home and told us about you. We've been searching for days."

"Geist?" asked Alphonsus.

"Our village. I'm sure it's not quite what you're used to, Your Highness, but we'll keep you safe."

"You live . . . *here?*" Esme asked. She cringed, looking around at the wasteland. "I thought the only inhabitants were those creatures."

Aharon shook his head. "Geist was settled long before those beasts showed up. We have the Hierophants to thank for them."

Esme, who'd been struggling to move under the weight of the children, looked up sharply. "What do you mean?"

Before Aharon could answer, Alphonsus drew in a long, loud breath. "Is that Geist?"

Just ahead, seven tall spires of chromium and glass jutted up over the tops of the canyon walls. They twinkled like stars in the daylight.

Aharon's face darkened. "No. That's Silberglas, the Hierophant city. Geist is close enough that the city protects us from the worst of the sandstorms that come through. It's more of a shield to us than anything."

Alphonsus fell in step next to the burly man. He couldn't keep himself from sneaking glances at Aharon's crossbow arm. *One of us*, Aharon had called Alphonsus. But he'd refused to explain more, saying only that the prince would understand once they got to Geist. Maybe he'd finally meet the clockmaker who could fix his clock. Or at least keep the numbers from vanishing.

They rounded a bend and got a much better look at Silberglas. Every structure glistened like the spires that had led them here. Alphonsus marveled at the rows of precious jewels that lined the edges of the glass streets. He found it hard to look directly at the crystalline and silver buildings, which reflected the sunlight like a beacon.

"There we are," Aharon said, gesturing with his crossbow. The prince turned his head to see the village of Geist. It was nothing like the beautiful city. A motley assortment of battered and torn yurts made of burlap and linen buttressed a rocky slope. The small village bustled with people pushing carts and carrying woven baskets. Nearly everyone he could see wore a mask similar to Aharon's, each painted with dark streaks and dots.

A sudden breeze shot through the village, ruffling the walls of the yurts and pelting people with flying sand, forcing everyone to stand in place. Nearby, a flat patch of land had been turned into a farming field where workers were tilling a plot of soil and gathering freshly ripened vegetables. It reminded Alphonsus of Somber End, only the people here worked even harder, to overcome the elements.

"Why don't you live in the city?" the prince asked Aharon.

"The Hierophant Collective would have left it protected," Esme explained, stepping to the edge of the silver city and staring up in admiration. "To keep outsiders from discovering their secrets. There are probably layers and layers of powerful charms to keep anyone who isn't a Hierophant from setting a single foot inside." To prove her point, she took a giant step forward and stood on one of the city's shiny streets.

Aharon folded his arms and frowned down at Esme. With a dancelike leap, he hopped from the dirt path they were on and landed next to her, within Silberglas's borders. He spun around and then hopped back out.

"Not exactly," he said with a grunt. "When the Hierophants abandoned their precious city, they left in a hurry. Didn't have time to add 'layers and layers' of anything. We can go in there anytime we want. But we don't."

"Why?" Alphonsus asked again.

"The Hierophants are the reason we're stuck here in the Hinterlands. We're not exactly eager to use anything that belonged to them. Although," he pointed to the village's crops, "we were grateful that they made the surrounding land fertile for farming. To serve their own purposes, of course."

Esme crossed back to the dirt path. "You said the Hierophants were responsible for the creatures that attacked us. What does that mean? And why are you stuck here? No one's forcing you to stay."

Aharon said nothing for quite some time. His shoulders slumped, and a look crossed his face that reminded Alphonsus of how his mother had looked immediately after the imperatrix had died.

"Many years ago," he finally said, very softly, "we fled the wars in our homeland. We built boats and crossed the seas. We settled here in the desert, where we could start over. We only wanted a simple life. Then, fifteen years ago, the Hierophant Collective appeared. They lifted their hands as one and pulled their *city* out of the earth. Soon other magic users followed. And they began doing terrible things. Things they didn't want anyone in Rheinvelt to know about."

Alphonsus gently put his hand on Esme's shoulder. He could feel her trembling with rage. He had no idea if she was angry at what Aharon was accusing the Hierophants of . . . or angry that she believed him. He guessed it was a little of both.

Aharon pointed to the village. "Our new home became our prison. We wanted to see if the imperatrix and empress of Rheinvelt would allow us to settle there. But we couldn't."

"Why?" Alphonsus asked. "You would have been given shelter."

Aharon leaned over and spoke quietly. "There's a creature out there. It roams the Hinterlands. Made of wind and terror."

"You mean the Leich—?"

Aharon clamped his hand over the prince's mouth. "Don't say its name. It can hear you say that word anywhere. And when you say the name, it comes. You don't want that. It behaves like an errant child, destroying everything in its path with a tantrum. It refuses to let any of us leave. We fight to survive every day. We've been trying to leave the Hinterlands since the Hierophants arrived. But the creature always finds us. We're stuck here."

"So," Esme said, her voice shaking, "the *creature* is why you're trapped here. It has nothing to do with the Hierophants."

Aharon raised a single eyebrow. "My dear, who do you think created that monster? For that matter, who do you think made the creatures that attacked you when you emerged from the cave? That's the handiwork of the Hierophant Collective, right there."

Alphonsus moved to stand between Esme and Aharon, but Esme brushed past him and threw her arms up in the air.

"You don't know what you're talking about! There's no way a Hierophant could have created that monster. It's impossible to use magic to create life."

"Well, I'm not here to quote your own laws to you, but I think you'll find that it's *forbidden* to create life. Not impossible. There's a difference. A big difference."

Esme looked ready to retort but then fell silent. She turned away.

Alphonsus, who'd grown up learning to defuse conflicts between the lords and ladies of the royal court when they got into heated discussions, did what he did best: he changed the subject.

"The children are wearing pendants. Esme says they're protective charms. Where did they come from?"

Aharon pulled at a thin chain around his own neck. It bore a similar triangle-shaped pendant. "The creature can't go near those of us who are wearing these. But it hurls boulders at us to keep us from leaving the wastelands."

"Why won't it let you leave?" Alphonsus asked.

"We don't know. We'd all have been killed long ago if it weren't for the Nachtfrau."

"Excuse me?" Esme had whirled around, her eyes wide with disbelief.

Aharon nodded. "She tried to smuggle us out of here, but the Hierophants stopped her. Instead, she gave these to us and made sure we're well protected. The Nachtfrau has protected all of Rheinvelt from that monster. I imagine you know all about her. She must be a hero where you come from."

"Well, now I've heard everything!" Esme pulled herself away from the children. "The Nachtfrau is no hero. You don't know her." With that, she turned and marched straight into Silberglas. Her image reflected and distorted on the shining buildings around her, getting smaller and smaller the farther she got.

"Esme!" Alphonsus called out.

"Let her go, lad," Aharon said gently. "There's no water in the city. She'll have to come back if she wants some. She needs time. I think I said a lot of things she wasn't ready to hear."

Aharon and the children led Alphonsus through the tent village. As the prince had suspected, nearly every person here was like him. Or rather, nearly every person was missing something from their bodies, which had been replaced with something else. He met a woman with a scythe for an arm. A man whose leg from the knee down was an armored boot. Some people had parts of them crafted from stone or glass. But no one else that he could see had a clock in their chest.

"Not everyone has a charm," the prince noted.

"The Nachtfrau gave them to us ten years ago. People have been born; people have died. We share the ones we have. If it's not your day to have a pendant, you stay close to Geist for your own protection."

Everywhere Aharon led him, Alphonsus was

welcomed with a warm smile and kindness. No one cared about the clock. No one cared he was a prince. They accepted him simply for who he was. He experienced a feeling unlike any he'd ever known.

Aharon took Alphonsus to the center of the village. Small dented cauldrons hung over a blazing firepit, and the scent of a sweet stew made the prince's stomach rumble. Wooden bowls and spoons were passed around. These strangers from another land raised their arms to the sky and leapt around in a vivid dance to praise the community meal and then got in line to be served.

Although everything about their existence felt meager, Alphonsus admired these people. *His* people. Now he knew. He'd come from a land overseas. He still had no idea why he'd been taken away or how he'd ended up in the walls of the imperial palace. Those answers, he hoped, would come later. There was something far more urgent he needed to address first.

"Aharon," the prince said, "I think we might be able to help each other. If I can destroy the Leich—the creature—will you and your people help me?"

The larger man's brow furrowed as if he was humoring Alphonsus. "We've tried fighting it. Believe me. It can't be beaten."

"You said your people fight every day. Well, that's what I need. I need fighters. I need an army. My empire is in danger, and I need to fight back against the man trying to take it over. Can you and everyone in Geist do that? If I destroy the creature."

Aharon gnawed on his lower lip. "I'd need to discuss it with the village. So many have given up hope. And they're tired of fighting. But for a chance to leave this place? I can't imagine anyone saying no." He gave the prince's shoulder a pat, then moved away, bellowing at the top of his voice that everyone needed to meet outside his tent.

Alphonsus felt his heart swell with confidence. After so many false starts, he saw a chance to return and reclaim his family's empire. He had a Hierophant on his side. He was about to marshal the most extraordinary army he could imagine. There was just one more thing he needed, the only thing he could think of that could possibly defeat the Leichleben.

He needed to find the Maiden.

28

The Lies

WELCOME TO SILBERGLAS.

Esme ignored the voice in her head. She was angry and confused, and wanted the solitude she'd had when she started this journey. She hadn't had a moment to herself in days. She needed to clear her head and think, but it appeared even that wasn't possible.

The young Hierophant walked up and down the streets of the beautiful city until the sun started to set. The glass and silver buildings took on an orange-and-pink aura in the twilight. She wondered again why the Collective had never told her about this place. She knew the story of the Hierophants' history in the mountainous country on the eastern border of Rheinvelt. She'd been told they led simple agrarian lives here. This glowing city of silver and glass was anything but simple.

A bit dustier than I remember. But I suppose that's to be expected.

"Leave me alone," Esme muttered. "Get out of my head. Stop looking through my eyes."

Oh, good. You've realized that spell works both ways. The blood ties of magic are amazing, aren't they? I'm just keeping an eye out for you. Mother's prerogative.

"I want my voice back," Esme said. She stared right into the silver door of the closest building, making sure the Nachtfrau could clearly see the anger on her face. She held up the infinitum box. "It's in here. Get it out."

Your voice is about so much more than the magic you wield. And it can be much more powerful than any single spell you cast.

"You didn't tell me the statue was *alive.*"

Was that important?

"No. It's not. Because the statue is gone now. I have no idea where it is. And I can't use magic to find it. If you want me to honor our agreement, give me my voice back so I can find the Maiden. I'll bring you the clock, you'll free the Hierophants, and I'll leave this horrible place."

The Nachtfrau remained silent for several moments. Then, in a voice that was both patient and exhausted, she said, *If you want to know how to get your voice back, you've already got the means to accomplish that. You only have to ask.*

"You want me to beg you? I won't do that," she said.

But the Nachtfrau didn't respond.

Esme continued exploring the lost city. She searched through what had once been someone's home. Sigils had been etched into the glass of nearly every wall and door, some acting as magical locks, others representing fortification to make the glass unbreakable. But, as Aharon had suggested, every place had been stripped bare of anything useful. What little remained—mostly furniture and decor—had been smashed, perhaps in an effort to make it useless to anyone who might stumble upon the city.

They really had left in a hurry. Esme had always been told the Hierophants left when the Nachtfrau became too powerful. They sought a land far from her ability to harm them. But, apparently, they'd underestimated her mother's reach. Esme was starting to believe there was no escaping the Nachtfrau.

Unless, of course, the Nachtfrau died. Which is what Esme had been sent to make sure happened in the first place. It became clear with every passing moment that she had to return to her original plan and kill the Nachtfrau. It was the only way Esme and the other Hierophants could be truly free.

As Esme wandered the city, she hoped to find something that might help her figure out how to release her voice from the box. Surely, if there were sigils she hadn't been taught by the Collective—like the binding sigils— there might be other types of magic here that she'd never seen before. The city had been a secret, after all. Maybe this was where the Collective had stored their most powerful magic.

But after hours of scouring the desolate glass buildings, she found nothing. No scrolls, no ancient texts. Nothing she could use.

You only have to ask, her mother had said. She'd assumed the Nachtfrau wanted Esme to ask her to break the spell that had taken Esme's voice. But what if that wasn't what she'd meant. What if she'd meant . . . ?

Esme reached into her sack and pulled out the infinitum box. It was dicey, but it was her best chance. She opened the lid and grimaced when the rhyme—the one that had so scared Alphonsus—came out in her own voice.

"How do I get my voice back?" she asked softly. What little vocal power she had was vanishing fast.

The box shuddered and breathed heavily. Then, her

own voice said strongly, "*Learn the truth.*" It paused, then continued with, "*Your voice will never return.*"

Esme's stomach sank when she heard the second response. It could be a lie . . . but what if it wasn't? She couldn't imagine living out the rest of her life not being able to perform magic.

And yet she had survived the past few days well enough. She'd done it without magic. She'd survived on her ability to think.

"Focus on the other answer," she told herself. "Learn the truth . . . learn the truth. What truth do I need to learn?"

She had forgotten that the box was still open. Responding to her question, the bone walls of the box vibrated, tickling her palms. Then her own voice said, "*Compassion is for the foolish and weak.*"

That certainly seemed true. She thought about all the times when her journey would have been simpler if she hadn't been compassionate. If she'd killed the white creatures in the Hinterlands. If she'd killed the Nachtfrau. Choosing mercy had certainly caused her many problems.

But then she thought of Alphonsus. She'd never met anyone as kind as him. Even when his compassion didn't necessarily help him, she felt that he'd still made the right choice.

The box quivered, and she held it close, hoping the

first answer had been a lie and that the answer still to come would be the truth that would help her get her voice back. But what the box said made the situation far, far worse. It said what she'd already started to suspect but didn't want to believe. It said what she'd come to fear most.

It said: *"Everything you believe is built on lies."*

29

Heart of Onyx

GUNTRAM STEINHERZ NO LONGER DREAMED OF WEALTH.
He no longer cared about respect or glory or power. All
those desires had been driven from his body as he lay at
death's door in the valley. There, he'd made silent bargains
with unknown forces, begging for a reprieve that would
spare him from dying at the Maiden's hand. He promised
he would never again seek the things he thirsted for as a
child, the things he begged the Maiden to give him. All
he wanted was one more chance at revenge. One chance
to destroy the person responsible for his fall.

And that chance had come from a creature com-
posed of more hate than Guntram would have imagined

possible. The creature made of tempest and desert waste—he knew its name now—had saved him. He felt the creature's anger when their minds joined. He basked in the Leichleben's fury. His dying wish had been granted. He not only had the opportunity to destroy Alphonsus; he also had the power to see it through.

Guntram had wandered the canyon for four days, lost in its seemingly endless stone warrens. He'd hoped that the enchanted onyx in his chest would guide him to the prince. But so far, he hadn't seen signs of any other life. Every so often, he heard the wild shrieks of the strange creature that had saved him. Even though their minds remained connected, the creature seemed of little value.

What Guntram did value was the lump of jagged onyx beating in his chest like a makeshift heart. He could feel it squirm in there, pumping raw fire through his veins with each jerk and twitch. He knew this was but a splinter of the Maiden, just a fraction of the vast power he assumed she wielded. Even still, it was more than enough. If his time with the Maiden had taught him anything, it was that the amount of power didn't matter as much as how you used what you had. Right now, he felt like he could do anything.

He'd had nothing to eat or drink since the creature

rescued him from the brink of death. The onyx alone—shaking with the combined power of the Maiden and the Leichleben—sustained him. It took away his need for sustenance and the desire to sleep. If the onyx couldn't guide him to the prince, it would empower him with the drive he needed to search every inch of the Hinterlands.

And search he would.

Guntram skulked down a long, narrow corridor of rough-hewn sandstone. The canyon walls above curved inward, creating a canopy that blocked out most of the light. As it grew dimmer, he swore he could see a dark-purple light pulse emanating from his chest. The onyx, letting him know it was there to serve.

But as he continued forward, a shadow fell across his path. He looked up, toward the end of the corridor, to see a familiar mammoth figure filling the pathway. Blocking his only way forward.

Turn back now, little boy. There are many paths you can take, but going home is the only one that ends well for you.

The Maiden's voice came from everywhere: the statue itself, the soil at Guntram's feet, just over his shoulder, and inside his own head. No. From inside his new onyx heart. The voice wasn't what the Margrave had expected, given her awful visage and the fact that her screams shattered glass. Her voice was low, husky, but also smooth and somewhat comforting.

"You're saying that because you're afraid," Guntram spat. "You know I can hurt you."

I'm saying it because this really is your last chance. Return to Somber End, put all this behind you. If you continue forward, you will never go home again.

"I am going forward. I'll kill that boy, the one you chose over me. And then, I'll grind *you* to powder."

The prince is protected in ways you'll never understand. That has been seen to. As for me, my strongest adversary on my worst day couldn't best me. What chance do you have?

Guntram took a step forward, sword drawn. The Maiden didn't move. But the flails of her cat-o'-nine-tails came to life on their own, slicing through the air and knocking the sword from the Margrave's hand.

He only laughed. "I have other ways to destroy you now."

He closed his eyes and raised his fist to the sky. The ground trembled. Cracks appeared up and down the canyon walls as people made of sandstone pulled themselves free. The stone figures—two dozen in all—trudged silently to stand at Guntram's side.

"So much power," Guntram said. "You had so much power, and all I wanted was just a taste of it. But you denied it to me, over and over, for ten years. Well, now it's mine. I took it from you!"

You didn't take it, little boy. It was given to you by mistake.

"Don't call me 'little boy'! If it's escaped you, I'm a man now. And I have power too."

No, Guntram Steinherz. You're still that little boy, curled up at my feet whispering wishes for power and wealth. I'm telling you now: your only chance of achieving your goals is to leave the Hinterlands.

Her words brought back the ridicule Guntram had endured at the hands of his own parents. He'd tried his best to earn their respect, maybe even their love. But they'd never given it. The Margrave understood now that he would also never get it from the Maiden. His anger ran cold as hopelessness and sorrow flooded every corner of his body.

"It didn't have to be this way," he whispered.

The Maiden's head jerked upward, and a pall of blackness fell all around them. Guntram couldn't see a thing. Groping in the darkness, he found one of the stone creatures he'd summoned and cowered behind it for protection. He reached for the dagger on his belt.

Then, slowly, light returned to the canyon. When he could see again, Guntram was alone with his creations.

The Maiden had vanished. Almost as if she'd never really been there. As if it had all been his imagination.

The stone warriors stood at the ready, waiting for orders. The Margrave knelt to retrieve his fallen sword. As he reached out, the sun set off a cascade of sparkles at the end of his arm, like stars twinkling against the night sky.

His entire hand had turned to onyx.

30

The Signal in the Tower

ALPHONSUS WAITED JUST OUTSIDE GEIST, CASTING THE occasional glance toward the bonfire around which Aharon and his people had gathered once dusk had settled. They were deciding right this very minute if they would help Alphonsus take back the empire. He wasn't sure what to do if they said no. But then, he wasn't sure what to do if Aharon and his people said *yes*.

The people of Somber End had turned on him. News of the prince's clock and his connection to the Maiden would spread beyond Somber End. Every village and town in Rheinvelt would grow to hate the prince, suspecting him of betrayal. There was a very real chance Alphonsus would have no choice but to spend the rest of his life here in the Hinterlands. A thought, he had to admit, that wasn't all that bad.

Still, he felt he had to fight for the empire. Or, perhaps, he just didn't want Guntram to win. This had become personal. He could bear losing the confidence of his people. But allowing the Margrave to ascend unchallenged? To usurp his mother's power? He'd never let that happen.

And even if Geist's refugees agreed to help, there was still the matter of finding the Maiden. If, in fact, she had survived the battle in the valley. Aharon's people had been unable to defeat the Leichleben. They *needed* the Maiden for that.

"I don't know if you can hear me," Alphonsus said to her, looking quietly to the night sky. "I sometimes feel you've *always* been able to hear me. I need you. More than ever. I'm scared. I guess that's nothing new. I know I need to start standing up for myself. But maybe if you could help just this one last time, I'll be brave the next time. Does that sound fair? If you're out there, please find me."

He paused and listened. Only the rush of the desert wind answered. He wasn't sure what he'd expected. He would have given anything to hear the statue call back *"Foot!"*

"Your Highness?"

Aharon stepped out from behind a tent. He bowed

low at the waist. "We would be honored to help you fight for your empire. If you can kill the creature, we'll gladly stand at your side."

Alphonsus felt relief and terror at the same time. More than anything, he feared the coming battle.

"Please thank your people," the prince said.

Aharon winked. "They're your people too, you know."

Alphonsus nodded. "You said earlier that I was definitely one of you. How could you be sure?"

The burly man crouched. "Two reasons. First, before the Nachtfrau's pendants, the creature tried to kill almost all of us. In fact, it nearly succeeded . . . but then it repaired us. The creature is very strange. It lashes out, and then, when it wounds someone, it attempts to fix them. That's how I got this." He held up the crossbow.

Alphonsus pressed his fingertips to the face of his clock. "This is from the Leich—creature?"

Aharon nodded. "Second . . . I knew your parents. I was there the night they were killed. The Hierophants had just vanished, releasing all the terrible monsters they'd created into the world. The creature attacked the village first. It was terrifying. It killed nearly everyone.

"It tore your parents' tent to pieces, killing them and almost killing you. And then it . . ."

"What?"

"I told you, it's very strange. Like a child who does

something wrong and knows it. If it were human, I'd say it tried to make up for what it had done. It brought you back to life with the clock. It used the debris from your house to make you a bassinet. Oh, how you cried. And then . . . you vanished. We never knew what happened to you."

The prince felt his breaths coming in short heaves. He wasn't the son of an incredible clockmaker. He was a product of the Leichleben. "Did it . . . Did it try to save my parents too?"

"I think it tried, but there are some things the creature learned it couldn't fix. It brought back what villagers it could and then left. That's when the Nachtfrau arrived and—"

"Aharon."

The voice that interrupted them was soft, and, if Alphonsus hadn't been distracted, he would have found it familiar. A person shrouded in a hooded cloak emerged from the darkness.

Aharon looked surprised. "You're back. I didn't think you'd be returning—"

"Things have changed," the woman said. "I was scouting along the south ridge. There's a new danger. A man with an army of stone creatures is getting close to the village. He's coming for the prince."

Alphonsus looked in the woman's direction. He

knew that voice. The woman stepped into the light and pulled back her cowl. Half of her body was made of clear glass. But otherwise, the prince recognized her as Birgit Freund.

"Hello, Your Highness," she said.

Alphonsus and Birgit sat across from each other at a wooden gable inside Aharon's tent. The leader of Geist had excused himself, leaving them to talk. They regarded each other a very long time.

The prince felt numb. He should have felt excited, thrilled even, to see the huntress again. But so much had changed since she'd gone. Alphonsus was no longer the boy who'd first sent Birgit on her mission. He thought of all the nights he'd waited anxiously for her return with news of the clockmaker who could save his life. He remembered desperately wanting just a word of how her quest was going. But he'd heard nothing in a year. And now, she just appeared from nowhere, as if the prince's worries didn't matter at all. As if nothing had changed. It made Alphonsus angry.

"You look well," Birgit said after an eternal silence.

"I waited for you," the prince replied. "I did what you told me, and I hung the lanterns in the tower to tell you that all was well."

Birgit closed her eyes and nodded. A small smile curved on her face. "Yes, that's right. It was a signal."

Alphonsus frowned. "You'd forgotten?"

"There's something I need to tell you, Your Highness." The huntress reached across the table, holding out her flesh hand. Alphonsus refused to take it. "This is going to be hard to hear and even harder to understand. I'm not the Birgit Freund you knew."

Alphonsus looked her up and down. Indeed. The Birgit Freund he knew wasn't half made of glass. "Who are you then?"

"I'm like you. I was cobbled together by that creature."

The pronouncement hung in the air like smoke from an extinguished candle. Alphonsus felt every inch of his skin go cold. His worst fear had come to pass.

"A couple months after Birgit left the palace," Glass Birgit continued, "she came to the Hinterlands, looking for the clockmaker you asked about. She was attacked by the creature and mortally wounded. It crafted this glass body to try to save her. But before it could finish helping her, she ran away. She managed to survive for several days, trying to get back to the palace. Finally, she collapsed just inside the Hexen Woods.

"The Nachtfrau found her. She could sense that Birgit was dying in the name of a great cause. Birgit's last thoughts were of you, Your Highness."

Alphonsus remained frozen in place. The back of his neck felt pinched as tears rolled down his cheeks. He swallowed, but his mouth had gone dry.

"The Nachtfrau did what she could. She pulled out the very best of Birgit: her memories, her love for her sister, your mother, and you. The Nachtfrau used these to animate me—for the sole purpose of telling you what you need to know. I apologize that it's taken so long. She told me to wait, saying I'd know exactly when the moment was right. I could have told you days ago, but I was the one who wasn't ready for the meeting then. It was selfish of me. I've enjoyed being Birgit. She was a good woman."

"Yes," Alphonsus said with fierceness.

Aharon pulled back the tent flap and stuck his head inside. "We've gathered all our weapons. I've asked everyone to get a good night's rest. It's just after midnight."

Alphonsus gasped and touched his clock. He looked down and watched as the number 3 faded away slowly. This time, he could feel it. It felt exactly the same as picking off a scab, exposing raw, soft flesh below. None of the other vanishing numbers had affected him before. The message was clear: his time was almost up.

Two days left. It would take that long at least to get back to the royal palace. And if Glass Birgit was right, the Margrave was now between him and home.

Glass Birgit stood. "Your Highness, I can help prepare

the village for battle. But it's important that we continue our conversation as soon as we set out."

Alphonsus nodded, and Glass Birgit left. The prince turned to Aharon. "Make sure everyone is ready to leave by midmorning."

Alphonsus barely slept that night. He'd been in the Hinterlands for over a week now and had never heard the wastelands as quiet as they were when he slept under the stars with these people. *His* people. Aharon and everyone he'd met here had been kind and generous. There had barely been any discussion about helping the prince. As one, the village had agreed to lay down their lives for him. Just as Birgit had done.

The prince decided he wouldn't let that happen again. Just before dawn, he packed as much food and water as he dared carry. He tiptoed out of the village and walked due west as quickly as possible. He couldn't stay. He couldn't go home. With what little time he had left, he was going to do what he did best.

Alphonsus ran.

31

Child's Play

"Are you there?"

It was maybe the twelfth time Esme had asked the question in the past few hours. Night had fallen, making it too dark to find her way back to Aharon's village of strange people. She sat on the balcony of an empty house, resigned to spending the night among the silver and glass. And because she herself couldn't cast the spell that activated the blood tie between her and her mother, she kept asking.

If the sorceress had cast the spell, she was keeping mum.

Esme didn't know if she could trust answers from the Nachtfrau. But at that moment, she wanted to hear *any* answers. Anything that could explain why Aharon was so insistent that the Nachtfrau was protecting them from the Leichleben. Anything that could explain exactly what she needed to do to get her voice back.

Anything that could tell her she hadn't believed an endless stream of lies her whole life.

Every single Hierophant had verified the stories of what the Nachtfrau had done—the destruction she'd caused, the fear she'd sown. They wanted Esme to know that she didn't have to follow her mother's evil path. She could choose to embrace what the Hierophants believed instead. And that, of course, was what Esme wanted to do.

But she also wanted to confront her mother. She wanted to ask why the Nachtfrau had done all those terrible things. Why consign the Hierophants to freeze to death when that very curse might have also killed her own daughter? Esme had learned enough now to know that there might be another side to the story. One she'd never imagined. One she wasn't sure she wanted to hear but also knew she had to.

"Mother!" she called out. "I know you can choose to hear me. If you hear me now . . . I want to talk."

Silence.

Furious, Esme pulled the infinitum box from her sack. "Talk to me, or I'll smash it!" She held it over her head, and when the silence continued, she threw the box over the balcony's edge. It hurtled toward the ground, but just before it struck the pavement, it shimmered and vanished from sight.

"No!" Esme screamed.

"Who's there?"

The voice was not that of the Nachtfrau. Esme peered over the edge of the balcony to find a robust woman bearing a torch in one hand and a sword in the other. She walked down the street, and something huge followed closely behind in the shadows, taking lumbering steps but remaining otherwise silent.

A wave of relief rippled through Esme at seeing the Maiden. Its left arm was missing, replaced by a trebuchet. When the Maiden spotted Esme, she stopped and tilted her head. With Esme on the balcony, the two stood eye to eye.

"Alphonsus is worried about you," Esme scolded the statue.

The Maiden hung her head in shame. "*Toe.*"

"Who's up there?"

Esme could see now that it was the woman who had claimed to be the prince's mother. Only now, she looked careworn and exhausted. There was a jagged rip in her breastplate, exposing a still-healing wound in the center of her chest.

"It's you," the empress said. "The girl."

"Are you really the empress? The prince's mother?"

Sabine nodded. "Where is my son? Is he safe?"

"He's not far. He's with . . . friends, I guess."

"Take me to him at once."

Esme made her way down and out of the house. "What's wrong?"

"The Margrave is getting closer. He's created soldiers of stone, and they're approaching this city from the south. I have to protect my son."

"You've got a light," Esme said, nodding to the torch. "We can find our way back to the village."

"What village?"

"The village where—"

Esme stumbled on the stone paving. The Maiden reached out to catch her. The instant they touched, the world around Esme fell away, as if all the glass in the city had shattered. The empress and Maiden had vanished. Esme was now standing in frozen tundra, barren and bleak. A familiar green glow—the northern lights—wriggled in the sky above. She panicked for a moment, thinking she'd returned to the North Lands and now had to start her journey all over again. But then she remembered, the Maiden was *very* enchanted, and enchanted items could retrieve lost memories. This was a memory of home. Nothing more.

But it *was* more. This was her dream. The dream she'd had hundreds of times since her father's death. The dream where her father filled the sky with magical sigils that glowed and sparkled against the backdrop of the northern lights. Which meant it had never been a dream. It had been real. This had all really happened.

Esme was reliving the moment, seeing everything through her own eyes as a child, just two years old. But the older Esme was merely there as a passenger. Young Esme was in complete control. She watched her father dance in place close by. Laughing, Young Esme danced too. Then Father lifted his right hand and drew a sigil in the air. Esme did the same. Father called out a cant. Young Esme repeated the word as best she could. And when she did, the sigil she'd drawn started to sparkle and hover in the air.

That was when Esme—the older Esme—noticed her father's left hand. His thumb and small finger touched to make an O. This was a simple gesture that every Hierophant knew. Gesturing with the left hand allowed you to practice drawing sigils and speaking their cants without the spell actually being cast. Nothing he did would result in a spell. But young Esme . . . she had no such limitation.

Esme felt light-headed and elated. He had been *teaching her magic.* Her earliest memories were of the Collective teaching her the cants and symbols. It had been her greatest regret that she'd never learned from her father.

But she *had*. This memory was proof.

Father continued dancing, drawing sigils, and singing out their cants. And young Esme imitated him exactly, matching his every gesture and sound. In moments, she had a dozen sigils sparkling over her head as Father laughed and cheered her on. Finally, he made a grand gesture. It was very complex, the hardest of everything he'd traced so far. He looked down into Esme's eyes and smiled.

"You can do this." His voice sounded slow and thick but as clear as anything. "We've practiced this."

Young Esme's small hand reached up and re-created the symbol precisely. She cried out the cant.

Suddenly, all the glowing sigils swirled around one another. Faster and faster until, all at once, they exploded in a shower of multicolored stardust, which rained down everywhere. Father scooped her up in his arms. "Well done!" he said, hugging her tightly. "Well done."

Father set her down, and as soon as her feet touched the ground, Esme fell and immediately found herself back in Silberglas. Just about everything unusual she'd seen since leaving the North Lands, she could blame on the Nachtfrau's tricks. But not this. The moment she entered the vision, she knew it had all been real. There was no way her mother could have done all this.

Her father had taught her to cast a spell long before the Collective had taken her under their tutelage. She'd had no idea that's what she was doing, of course. To young Esme, it had just been a game. But now, the horror of what she'd seen stuck. That hadn't been just any spell she'd cast. She knew now—having seen those same sigils carved into the canyon walls—that her father had had been showing her how to cast a binding spell. She'd guessed a while ago that the symbols on the walls were what kept the Leichleben in the Hinterlands, preventing it from leaving here and attacking Rheinvelt. Binding sigils kept something from leaving. Like the Hierophants in the North Lands.

Sabine dropped her torch and sword, racing to catch Esme as the girl collapsed at her feet. The young Hierophant's world went dark as she realized for the first time what had really happened all those years ago. The Nachtfrau hadn't confined the Hierophants to the North Lands.

Esme had.

Point of No Return

GUNTRAM FLICKED HIS WRIST. JAGGED CRACKS SPLIT THE ground, and a creature of clay and dust rose up, pulling itself away from the dry earth. It stood upright and silently fell in line with the other mindless soldiers the Margrave had created. He was up to fifty now. He didn't imagine he'd need them all to bring down the prince. But then, he also hadn't imagined that killing a young boy would be this difficult in the first place. To be on the safe side, he flicked his wrist again and another stone creature pulled itself from the canyon stone and joined the march.

Guntram's walking had slowed considerably. The onyx that had consumed his right hand had now taken the whole arm. The same for his entire left leg. While they still bent as easily as his flesh limbs, the stone was heavier and required all his strength to maneuver. But with each part of him that joined his new onyx heart, he felt his power grow. When he closed his eyes, he could feel that he was getting closer to finding Alphonsus. Closer and closer . . .

This is your last chance, Guntram Steinherz. The point of no return. You can still save yourself if you give up your pursuit. You've been using magic. And there's always a Balance.

He couldn't see the Maiden, but her voice rang as loudly in his head as if she'd been standing right next to him. Guntram laughed.

"You're afraid of me," he replied. "You can feel how powerful I'm getting. Remember my promise: when the prince is dead, I'm coming for you next."

I'm sorry, Guntram, the Maiden said. *I'm sorry you feel you wasted your time all those years ago. I'm sorry I let you down. I didn't understand how much you wanted power.*

Guntram had not been prepared for the statue to apologize. It was more than he'd ever gotten from his parents. But now that the Maiden had said the words, Guntram didn't know what to do with them. Was an apology good enough? He wanted it to be. The part of him that was still the small boy sitting at the base of the statue ten years ago wanted all to be right again, even after everything that had happened. He wanted to forgive her. But his anger wouldn't let him.

"You didn't understand?" Guntram screamed. "I told you everything! I begged. I pleaded for you to help me. When I was summoned to the palace to serve the empress, I thought you were granting my wishes. But that was all a mistake, wasn't it? You never intended for me to succeed. You would have been happier if I'd spent the rest of my life telling you my secrets and begging you for help."

If it means anything, I think I finally understand what it is you want. I can never make things right, but I may be able to set you on the path toward what you desire.

Something twinkled in the air above Guntram's head as a small white box fell from the sky and landed softly in the sand at his feet. The Margrave picked it up with his onyx hand. A wave of pure energy passed through him. This box made the power he got from the onyx in his body look like a candle compared to the sun.

He studied the box with its gray-white bone walls and strange glyphs carved into every surface. Cautiously, he flipped the lid open. The box breathed deeply, and the voice of a woman rose out of it.

"When nights pass as hours the same
The end of time will start

A sacrifice is all that saves
The counterclockwise heart"

Guntram scowled. "What is this?"

The box jerked in his hand. Another breath wheezed from inside and the woman's voice said, *"I am a Hierophant grimoire, capable of storing an unlimited number of spells for future use."* The box paused and then said, *"I am an infinitum box, repository of all knowledge. I speak one lie and one truth to any question asked."*

Why would the Maiden give this to him? If it was either of the things it claimed, he would be more powerful than the statue itself. He didn't trust the Maiden. However, there was an easy way to test the box.

"What do I want more than anything?" he asked.

The box answered, *"To destroy Prince Alphonsus and the Onyx Maiden."* A pause, and then, *"To be the greatest baker in Somber End."*

So it *was* an infinitum box. And it would answer any question. He only had to decide which answer was a lie and which was the truth.

"Where is Prince Alphonsus?" he asked, his mouth slick with anticipation.

The box remained quiet for several moments. Then it replied, *"Continue north for half a day's journey. You will find the prince outside the city of Silberglas."* And after another moment, it said, *"The prince has returned to the royal palace and is marshaling a force to hunt you down."*

Guntram considered. One of these answers was a lie. He couldn't imagine the prince returning home. The people of Somber End were terrified of him, believing him to be an acolyte of the Maiden. So the first answer seemed more likely.

He picked up the box and, just for good measure, created two more stone monsters to join his party. Together, the Margrave and his soldiers traveled due north, as the box had suggested. When the sun was halfway to the horizon, they climbed a hill and rounded a ridge. Guntram looked down. Just ahead, the silver and glass spires of a city peeked out over the tops of the canyon walls.

Guntram stared at the glistening towers. He opened the lid of the box, waited for it to finish speaking the rhyme, and then asked very clearly, "Tell me: Exactly how do I destroy Prince Alphonsus?"

33

The Last Lesson

ALPHONSUS WALKED UNTIL HIS LEGS COULD BARELY HOLD him. He guessed he'd traveled deeper into the Hinterlands than anyone in Rheinvelt had ever gone. He wasn't even sure if this could be considered the Hinterlands anymore. He'd exited the canyons at midday and trekked across the bleak, flatlands beyond. The gray earth was dry, cracked clay. No trees. No plants. No animals. Absolutely nothing as far as the eye could see.

Well, not exactly nothing.

"Leave me alone."

Alphonsus had known he was being followed almost immediately upon leaving the village. He'd briefly considered tricking his pursuer, but he knew he'd never be able to fool a master tracker.

Glass Birgit had kept far behind and done her best to hide her pursuit. But now that they were out in the open, she'd closed the distance until she walked only a few lengths behind the sullen prince.

"I hope it means something," she called ahead to him, "that Birgit's last thoughts were how she'd failed you."

"You have her memories, and you ignored me for a year," Alphonsus called back over his shoulder. "You could have returned to the palace any time after Birgit died and told me what had happened."

"I'm afraid it's more complicated than that. The Nachtfrau is a very powerful sorceress. No one can see the future—not even the soothsayers who claim they can—but the Nachtfrau knew the empire was in danger. She could see all the pieces moving, like on a giant chessboard. She had to guess which moves to make to protect as many people from the oncoming chaos as she could. I helped her set up her countermoves. I did it to protect you, which was more important than coming back and breaking your heart."

The prince spun around and faced the huntress down. "*Someone* can tell the future. *Someone* has known what was going to happen to me." He pointed to his backward-running clock. Then he threw back his head and screamed the mysterious rhyme as loudly as he could. "I've been haunted by those words my entire life, telling me that I'm going to die. I tried to stop it, and I failed. So I give up. I'm going to walk until the last number on my clock disappears, and it'll all be over."

Glass Birgit folded her arms and arched her crystalline eyebrow. "I taught you better than this, Alphonsus."

"*You* didn't teach me anything. You said it yourself: You're not the real Birgit. She's dead. She died because . . . because I sent her to find someone who doesn't exist. All to save my own life!"

As if pulled down by invisible weights, the prince finally gave in to his fatigue and dropped to his knees on the desert floor. He bowed his head and sobbed.

The huntress crossed her legs and lowered herself next to him. "You're right. I'm not the real Birgit. I wish I were. I've wished it every day since I was created. She loved you so much. Like her own son. And I may not be her, but I feel her love for you."

She reached out with her flesh hand and lifted his chin until their eyes met. "Your clock may be running backward, but your heart has never done that. Your heart has never once turned against those you love and what you believe. You are filled with more compassion than anyone I've ever known. The fact that you're here, trying to draw the Margrave's army away from the village, is evidence of that. Our world would be so much brighter if more people could care as powerfully as you, Your Highness."

Alphonsus leaned in and put his arms around the huntress. The glass half of her body was smooth and cool to the touch. But he accepted it as part of her now. He accepted her as Birgit. And he felt ashamed that he'd ever thought of her otherwise.

"Back at the village, you said you had one more lesson to teach me."

"Yes. I'm sorry it's taken this long—"

"Don't apologize. What's the lesson?"

Birgit paused. For a second, Alphonsus thought it looked as if she'd changed her mind and wouldn't tell him. Then she said, "She wanted to tell you . . . *I* want to tell you it was a privilege to know you. And teach you. The final lesson is this: There are things you learn. And there are things you are told. Sometimes, they're the same. Sometimes, they're not. When they're the same, pay attention. When they're not the same, pay *more* attention."

Alphonsus repeated the words back exactly. Then he said, "I don't understand."

"You will. I promise. I know you don't always have faith in what you can do, Your Highness, but I've never doubted you once."

He sighed. "You don't know me, Birgit. Not who I

really am. I'm a coward. I've always been afraid. All I do is run."

"No. I've always known exactly who you are. There's nothing wrong with being afraid. Being brave is so much more than raising a sword and charging into battle. It's being afraid but still doing what's right. No one does that better than you."

Birgit flinched and clenched her jaw. Alphonsus looked up and noticed that the glass on the one side of her face was spreading to the other. Slowly but surely, the soft olive skin cleared away, leaving sparkling glass.

"What's happening?" Alphonsus asked.

The huntress smiled weakly. "The enchantment that kept me going since Birgit's death was powered by her desire to impart that knowledge. Now that I've done it, I've served my purpose. We have to say goodbye, Your Highness."

A sound like ice cracking on a lake accompanied the glass as it continued to take over Birgit's whole body.

Alphonsus looked ready to protest, but Birgit took both his hands. "We can't stop it. Just go . . . find . . . the empress."

"My mother?"

"She's close. Go back . . . to . . . the village . . ."

Birgit's words came out crackling, until she could no longer speak. Alphonsus held her hands tightly until at last she was made entirely of glass. Birgit froze with a loving smile on her face.

The ground beneath the prince shifted. Starting with her feet, Birgit began to turn to sand. The huntress melted and melted until she was nothing more than a waist-high pile of sparkling dust.

Alphonsus wiped his tears with the back of his hand. Then he took a deep breath and turned in the direction from which he'd come. The Margrave and his stone army were getting closer. And there was only one person standing between them and the village.

"Mother."

34

The Truth

Esme awoke in a broken bed. As her bleary eyes adjusted, she looked around. The glass walls of the house reflected pink and orange, meaning the sun was either rising or setting. She saw the balcony where she'd been standing.

She smacked her dry lips and turned to find the empress of Rheinvelt seated in the room's one unbroken chair, waiting patiently. Esme glanced out the window, looking for the Maiden. The statue was nowhere to be seen.

"I think your body is saying you needed some rest," the empress said. "You've been asleep almost an entire day."

"You stayed with me all night?" Esme asked softly. "I would have thought you'd be out looking for your son."

"You told me he was safe," Sabine replied. "It didn't seem like *you* were. It felt more important to make sure you were well."

Esme pressed at her temples. A slight headache throbbed just behind her eyes. But as she grew more awake, the pain faded. "Thank you."

"So, what did you see?" Sabine asked. "I'm assuming you saw something when you touched the Maiden? When I touched her, I saw . . . that she's been very diligent in watching over my empire. I saw that she's been misjudged, by others but by none more than me. When we touched, it created a connection. Something I don't understand. Is it the same with you?"

Esme searched her mind. She could feel no connection to the Maiden. "No. But . . . yes, I saw things. True things."

The empress didn't press for more information. She placed her hand on top of Esme's, as if knowing the girl needed it.

Esme sat up and allowed the empress to help her take a drink of water from her canteen. "Alphonsus has told me a lot about you. We were lost in these caves for days, and he wouldn't stop talking about how much he missed you and . . . You seem like an amazing mother."

Sabine smiled. "I'm sure your mother is amazing too."

"I never really knew my mother. I've only known . . . *about* her. My mother is the Nachtfrau."

"The evil sorceress who lives in the Hexen Woods?"

Esme's face flushed with embarrassment. She'd never admitted this to anyone outside the Hierophants. Not even Alphonsus. "I'd understand if you hated me because of everything my mother's done. I'm sure she's terrorized Rheinvelt for years."

"You know . . ." The empress stroked her chin. "I can't say that she has. Rumor has always been that she was terrible and would curse anyone who entered the woods. But I don't know that it ever actually happened."

"The Collective—the Hierophants elders who raised me—taught me about all the awful deeds my mother's done. Stories that gave me nightmares. I'm . . . starting to realize that maybe some of it wasn't exactly true. I think . . . I think it was the Collective that spread the rumor that the Nachtfrau was evil. To keep people from going to her." *To keep people from learning the truth*, she added in her thoughts.

The empress helped Esme to her feet and took the girl by the arm. "I won't pretend to understand what sort of cruel people turned a girl's heart against her own mother. But I know what it means to believe stories without proof. I've been told for years that the Onyx Maiden was evil and would destroy us all someday. But I've seen for myself that nothing could be further from the truth. I guess some stories are just stories until you learn otherwise."

Esme wanted to trust the empress. She almost let it all spill out. How she'd been sent to murder her own mother. How she knew the need for that murder was based on a lie. Or a misunderstanding. She wasn't sure which. But clearly, she had a lot more to learn.

Outside, the soft rumble of stone-on-stone footfalls vibrated through the glass floors. A moment later, the Maiden's terrifying face appeared in the window near the balcony.

"*Foot!*" she announced in greeting.

"I can take you to Alphonsus now," Esme told the empress. "It shouldn't take long—"

"I'm afraid we don't have time," Sabine said. "The Maiden tells me that the stone army has breached the southern gates of the city. They're coming this way."

"You . . . got all that from 'Foot'?"

The empress smiled. "As I said, the Maiden and I . . . share a connection. I don't understand it. But we work well together. And we're going to head off the soldiers. With any luck, they'll never make it to the village."

"What should I do?"

"You're a Hierophant, yes? Please, go to my son and use your magic to protect him. If I fail to stop the Margrave and his monsters, you'll be the last line of defense. I only hope it doesn't come to that."

"But I can't . . ." Esme stopped. She looked down at her fingers. They'd been useless for days. Unless of course . . .

The girl nodded. "I'll keep Alphonsus safe. No matter what."

The empress kissed Esme on the forehead, drew her sword, and climbed onto the Maiden's shoulder from the balcony. Together, they marched off to face the stone monsters.

Esme returned to the street. She thought of the memory of her and her father. The night she'd unknowingly bound the Hierophants to the hellish frozen glacier that would soon kill them all. Whose idea had it been for the Hierophants to tell her the Nachtfrau had bound them? How could the Collective spend Esme's lifetime convincing her that her own mother was evil when nothing Esme had witnessed for herself could verify that?

Her heart sank. She'd been ignoring the truth. She *knew* why.

Her fingers traced two sigils over her head, and she shouted their cants. Her voice rang out strong and sure. The glowing sigils fell to the ground, forming a whirlpool of golden light at her feet. The light spun faster and faster until it stretched out, forming an arrow that lit a path through Silberglas's twilight-coated streets. The arrow would lead her directly to Alphonsus.

And she started to cry. The tears poured out and seemed like they would never stop. She couldn't remember the last time she'd cried. Or if she'd ever cried. Her chest tightened, and she allowed a single low wail to fill the empty street around her. She cried and cried.

Because being able to use magic again meant she now knew the truth.

And that truth was this: everything she'd believed—about her mother, the Collective, and her whole life—had been a lie.

35

Prophecy

THE FULL MOON SHONE BRIGHTER THAN ALPHONSUS HAD
ever seen it. Its pearl-colored light guided him across the
desert plains back to the edge of the canyon. He could just
make out the shiny outline of Silberglas, hidden behind
the sandstone walls.

The Barefoot Prince stood at the canyon's entrance. If
he walked all night, he'd make it to Aharon's village by
sunrise. He rubbed his fingertips against the two remaining numbers on his clockface. *Brrda-tick-click, brrda-tick-
click.* There was a very real chance the last number would
vanish before all this was over. He had no idea what that
meant and, for the first time ever, he didn't care.

A flicker of golden light appeared just ahead in the

canyon. It raced along the ground, getting closer and closer. Alphonsus started as the glow stretched out from the canyon and stopped just short of his toes. The tip of the light formed an arrowhead. When he stepped to the side, the arrow turned in his direction. When he leapt into the air, the arrow lifted, following him up and then down. Someone knew where he was.

It wasn't long before Esme stepped from the canyon and into the moonlight. "You found your voice," the prince said with a smile.

But Esme didn't smile back. "Alphonsus, something's happening."

"I'm sorry Aharon upset you. It was rude of him to say those things about the Hierophants."

"No, everything he said was true. But listen. Your mother sent me to protect you. She said the Margrave was coming with an army of stone creatures."

"I know. Birgit told me. Where's Mother?"

"She and the Maiden have gone to face the stone army."

Alphonsus felt his hands go cold. His mother and the *Maiden*? How had they found each other? It was his mother who'd told him stories of the Maiden being something awful, something meant to bring doom to all of Rheinvelt.

But that's what she'd *told* him. He'd *learned* something very different. Birgit's final lesson rang home.

"I'm glad you're safe, Esme. And I'm glad you can use magic again. But I don't need you to protect me. It's probably best if we part ways now. I don't know what brought you to Rheinvelt, but I know you didn't come to die defending someone else's empire. Go home."

He walked past her. Esme stood there, looking stunned.

"Alphonsus, where are you going?"

"To Aharon's village." He tried to keep walking, but she gripped his wrist.

"No. That's where the Margrave is going. If I'm to protect you, we need to be as far from there as possible."

"But I promised to help them. I need the Maiden to kill the Leich—the creature."

Esme took him by the shoulders. "You're not listening to me. I promised your mother I'd keep you safe. I don't know who this Margrave is, but he's not going to stop until he kills you. For all you know, *this* is what the rhyme was talking about." She tapped the clock in his chest. "This could be counting down the moment until the Margrave kills you. If I can keep you away from him until the last number vanishes, we can stop the prophecy from coming true."

Alphonsus waited for the mention of his death to bring back his lifelong fear. It didn't.

"No."

The prince had never sounded so sure. Esme stared back in disbelief.

"What prophecy, Esme? You mean that rhyme? The one etched on my bassinet? The one your box repeats every time it opened? We don't know what it means."

"I think it's very clear," Esme argued. "The only way to save you is for someone to make a sacrifice. You can't want that."

"Of course not. But that was just something I was *told*. What I've *learned* is it's okay to be scared if you still do what's right. I'm done running. And no one is sacrificing anything to save me."

Esme stood quietly. She drew a sigil with her finger, whispered, and the arrow at the prince's feet vanished. They stared at each other in the moonlight, neither sure what to say next.

"You want to know why I came to Rheinvelt?" Esme asked.

Alphonsus nodded. "Yes, please."

The young Hierophant explained it all, starting with the fact that the Nachtfrau was her mother and that she'd been sent to kill the sorceress.

Alphonsus listened carefully. "Do you think you could have killed her?"

"I don't know. It's become obvious that magic won't solve all my problems. I'd like to think I'm not the spoiled child my mother thinks I am. But I probably am. If I ever see her again, I'll have to ask."

"Okay, then. We only have to survive this and you'll get a chance."

"Survive what?"

"We're going back to the village. And we're going to face what comes next."

Esme shook her head. "I told your mother I'd protect you. And even without the stone army, there's still that creature that—" She stopped. She looked to the horizon for several moments. "No, wait. I . . . I think I have an idea how to handle the creature."

"Perfect." Alphonsus said. "And there's one other thing I need from you . . ."

36

The Final Miracle

Esme and Alphonsus reached the village shortly after sunrise. Aharon and the villagers scrambled about. They piled up every wheelbarrow, fence post, and plow they could find around a single yurt, fortifying it. Children were ushered inside the round tent while the adults took up arms and stood guard. Aharon spotted the prince and the young Hierophant.

"Where have you two been?" he demanded, shaking a crude spear at them.

"What's happening?" Esme asked.

Aharon pointed his spear toward the glass city. "Can't you hear?"

Esme turned her head. Somewhere, in the streets of

Silberglas, the sounds of battle tore through the air. She could make out the Maiden's fierce roars and the unmistakable clangs of weapons hitting their marks. And with every second that passed, the sounds got closer.

"It looks like your war has come to us, Your Highness," Aharon said. "Are you ready to lead?"

Esme and Alphonsus exchanged looks. "Actually," the prince said, "by my authority as a member of the imperial family, I'm making a battlefield commission and naming Esme as our general-in-chief."

Esme smirked. "Can you do that?"

"Well, I've done it," Alphonsus replied with a shrug. "Can't turn back now."

The prince reached for Aharon's spear. "May I?"

The village leader handed his weapon to the prince, who nodded to Esme and then headed for the south end of the village.

"Where's the prince going?" Aharon asked.

"He's got something to do," Esme said. "And so do I."

Aharon shook his head. "We all need to prepare. The Margrave's army will be here any minute."

"I believe Prince Alphonsus promised he'd end your imprisonment here in the Hinterlands, yes?" Esme said. "We need to take care of that."

"But the army—"

"I'm sure the empress and the Maiden have it under

control." Esme turned around, cupped her hands around her mouth, and shouted, "Leichleben!"

The villagers gasped. Some cowered. Others ran into the fortified yurt, hoping to hide.

"What are you doing?" Aharon shouted. "You'll get us all killed!"

"You all wear protective charms," the young Hierophant replied. "The Leichleben can't touch you."

Aharon gripped Esme by the shoulders and pulled her close. "It doesn't need to touch us to kill us."

With a shriek, the storm of dust and shadows appeared. The Leichleben howled and tore into everything in its path, shredding tents and hurtling timber everywhere like missiles. As the creature ripped through the village, two oxen flew into the air, crashing down on the yurt where all the villagers had been hiding. Everyone inside screamed as their only protection collapsed around them, preventing them from fleeing.

"Help me, girl!" Aharon threw himself at the yurt's ruins, tearing at the walls to reach the people trapped under the debris.

But Esme's focus stayed on the approaching monster. If she used magic to help Aharon, the Balance could prevent her from dealing with the creature.

The young Hierophant stepped around the destroyed yurt, placing herself between the trapped villagers and the creature. The Leichleben's roar thundered in Esme's chest as it barreled toward her. Esme balled her hands into fists, fighting her instinct to defend herself with magic. She braced herself as the shadowstorm bore down, its winds forcing her to dig her feet into the ground so she wouldn't fall over.

"No."

She said it loudly and firmly. As the Leichleben continued approaching, she said it again.

"No!"

The creature stopped. It churned in place, kicking up dust as a low growl rumbled at the center of its vortex. It continued to thrash about, shrieking. But, as Esme had suspected, it had listened.

"You don't get to be angry when someone uses your name," Esme told the creature.

It roared and lashed out with a tendril of sand, uprooting a small garden. Esme held up a single finger and fixed the Leichleben with a stern glare.

"I know you're very upset." She spoke calmly, soothingly. She almost didn't recognize her own voice. "You've been alone all these years. It's why you wouldn't let these people leave the Hinterlands. You wanted someone else here with you."

"But it tries to kill us," Aharon hissed.

"It's confused. It was never taught any better. And it's

so, so lonely. I can't imagine what that's like." She took another step toward the Leichleben. "The Hierophants abandoned you. I'm sorry about that."

The Leichleben stopped rumbling. It hovered in place as if it wasn't quite sure what to do with Esme. The fierceness of its winds subsided; the tendrils of sand hung limply at its side. The creature's spherical shape began to wobble, as if ready to collapse.

Aharon approached slowly from behind, his crossbow aimed at the monster. "What are you doing?"

"You said it yourself. The Hierophants made the Leichleben. They broke their own laws and created life. Not just life . . . A child. They created a child, gave it power over life and death, and did nothing to help it understand itself."

Esme took a step toward the creature. Aharon groaned, but she quickly shushed him.

"I want to help you," Esme said softly to the creature. "There's so much I can help you understand. About who you are. Where you came from. Would you like that? Everything is going to be all right."

The Leichleben thrashed but otherwise fell silent.

"You can't hurt people anymore," Esme said. "It's okay to be angry sometimes. But I can teach you so much more. Do you understand . . . Leichleben?"

The creature let out something that sounded like a

whimper and shook for a moment. But Esme stood her ground, hands on her hips.

A woman from the village put her arm around Aharon. "It's a miracle. This girl performed a miracle."

"How did you do that?" Aharon asked.

"It never had a mother," she replied. "I know what that's like. I just said what I hoped my mother would say to me." And in case her mother was listening, she thought, *Did I get it right?*

If the Nachtfrau had been listening, Esme never knew. At the exact moment the young Hierophant reached out with her thoughts, she felt a sharp sting in the small of her back. When Esme looked down, she saw the point of a stone sword sticking out of her stomach.

Before she hit the ground, a single stone warrior stepped from the shadows of Silberglas, a bloody sword in its hand.

Esme choked, tears welling in her eyes. She'd misunderstood her role in all this. But now, it was clear. *A sacrifice . . . is all . . . that saves . . .*

Power

AHARON'S VILLAGE WAS FAR BEHIND ALPHONSUS NOW. Several hours' walk at least. There was no one he could ask for help when the time came. And strangely, he found comfort in this thought. He knew that the only way to solve his problem was to do it on his own terms. At least, that's what he hoped.

"A coward to the very end, I see."

Alphonsus stopped. Just ahead, Guntram stepped out from behind a rock. He looked very different than the last time the prince had seen him. Most of the Margrave's body was now made of onyx. Small bits of flesh—his right cheek, a bit of forehead and eye—stuck out. One leg moved more smoothly than the other, suggesting it was unchanged. But the rest of him looked like he could be the Maiden's lost twin.

"You're a long way from the battle, Margrave."

"I received a very good piece of advice," Guntram said, holding out the infinitum box. "I was told that if I sent my stone army to attack the city as a diversion, you would try to escape to the south. Turns out that was right. And here we are. No Maiden. No Hierophants. Just the two of us."

Alphonsus held up his spear. "Killing me won't fix anything," he said. But Guntram only laughed.

"I should let you live," the Margrave said, his voice booming and hollow. Much lower than it had ever been. "It's clear you'll never be a real threat to me. You're always too afraid to face your problems."

"I'm here now," Alphonsus said. It took all his strength just to squeak out those few words. "I'm facing you now."

Guntram's eyes narrowed. "You knew I'd be here?"

"I hoped. My teacher taught me to think like my enemy. She told me to consider the last thing they'd do . . . and then assume they'd do it. But, she said, that only works when your enemy isn't very smart."

The Margrave drew his sword. "I don't understand what the Maiden saw in you. And I never will." He leapt, thrusting the sword forward. Alphonsus easily deflected the clumsy blow with his spear.

"I don't understand either," the prince admitted. "But I think you *do* care. I think everything that's happened is because you care too much about what the Maiden thinks of me. Or doesn't think of you. Have you always cared too much what others think of you, Margrave?"

Before Guntram could strike again, Alphonsus held up a long, smooth stone. He showed the Margrave the stone's flat side, on which Esme had carved a beautiful whorl. Guntram's one flesh eye widened in recognition.

"It's full of magic," Alphonsus said. "You can feel that, right? You can have this and all the magic inside. I know that's what you want. But I should warn you: touching enchanted items can have side effects."

The prince tossed the stone at Guntram, who snatched it greedily. The moment the stone touched the Margrave's flesh, the canyon walls around them melted like charcoal etchings left in the rain. The landscape reshaped and reformed until the pair found themselves in an unkempt single-room house. Dirty, threadbare curtains hung from the windows. An unmade, lumpy bed sat in one corner. In the opposite corner, a smattering of hay and a tatterde-malion blanket suggested another bed of sorts. The dirt floors—covered in moldy food scraps clinging to bone, broken dishes, and trash—suggested that no one had ever cleaned.

Guntram shot a look of horror at Alphonsus.

"It's just a memory," the prince said. "*Your* memory. We're not really here."

Guntram shrank, the onyx parts of his body returning to flesh, until he was once again an eleven-year-old boy. The boy sat sullenly at a table next to a bowl of broth that stank of sour milk and spoiled cabbage.

The door to the house flew open, and a man—unshaven, with wrinkled clothes and a wild look in his eye—stormed inside.

"There he is!" the man declared.

Guntram flinched. He wouldn't meet the man's eye.

"Our great storyteller. Home again from another wasted day talking to a pile of stone." The man sneered. It was clear he knew how much he scared the boy. And he enjoyed every minute of it.

"That's not true, Father," young Guntram said. "The harvests have been bountiful again. Somber End's misfortunes have turned around—"

Guntram's father threw a ceramic cup that just narrowly missed his son's head, smashing on the wall behind. "Of course you think that has something to do with you. Don't be stupid! The crops have good years and bad years. It's always been that way. People who think that statue is affecting our fortunes are idiots. And only idiots think talking to stone will change anything."

Guntram lowered his head but didn't say a word as his father snatched the bowl of broth away. "Look at this. We eat filth. You should be working, bringing in money for the family. But you've convinced everyone in town that what you do is important. Well, it's not. It's not important at all. And it doesn't bring us money. And you know what that means? It means you're worthless. *Worthless.*"

The boy threw back his head and screamed. The room vanished, returning the Margrave and prince to the canyon. Young Guntram shed his skin like a snake, revealing the adult nearly onyx man once again.

Alphonsus stood over Guntram, who sobbed on all fours. "Margrave—"

"Don't say a word!" Guntram spat.

Alphonsus understood. He'd let his fear of the Margrave blind him to a simple fact. When Guntram came to live in the imperial palace, the prince had been *told* he was a wise man. But what Alphonsus had *learned* was that Guntram was scared. Just like the prince. Only Guntram had allowed his fear to become anger.

"My old teacher told me I was the most compassionate person she knew," the prince said. "But I've realized she was wrong. I've tried to care about everyone. But I withheld my compassion from the people who needed it the most. I understand you now, Margrave. I'm sorry."

Guntram howled, sounding very much like the Maiden before she attacked. "Do *not* pity me, you brat! You understand nothing."

The Margrave swung his sword wildly. Alphonsus backed away, showing no fear.

"You did your best to help Somber End," the prince said. "Your parents may not have appreciated it, but you know the village did. You know they saw you as their guardian."

"I meant nothing to them. The fact that I was so easily replaced by a freak like you proves that."

Guntram faked to the left, then spun around and sliced the sword into the prince's upper arm. Alphonsus cried out and fell backward to the ground.

"When you're dead," Guntram said with a growl, "the Maiden will understand that she never should have picked you. She'll know that her power should have been mine. No one will doubt me ever again."

The Margrave raised the sword high above his head. Alphonsus closed his eyes, knowing Guntram was right. He could never really understand everything the Maiden's original guardian had been through.

"Aaahhh!"

Alphonsus grimaced as pain shot through his chest. He opened his eyes, assuming Guntram had run him through with the sword. Instead, he watched as the number 1 faded from sight on his clockface. All three of the clock's hands came to a full stop at the top, where the number 12 should have been. A sizzling sound rent the air. The remaining flesh parts of the Margrave solidified and grew dark in an instant. He froze in midstrike, unmoving as a statue, now fully onyx.

Alphonsus stared up at Guntram, wondering if the Margrave was even in there anymore. He stood cautiously, waiting for the statue to resume its attack. It didn't.

He looked down at his clock. All the numbers had returned. And the second hand was ticking forward once more. He hadn't died. The countdown had never been for him. But if not for him, then for whom?

"I'm sorry, Guntram," Alphonsus said. "I'm really sorry." Head bowed, the prince turned and made his way back to Geist.

38

Guntram

THIS IS IT, GUNTRAM. THIS IS WHAT IT MEANS TO HAVE INFI-nite power. This is the ability to make your every heart's desire come true. Can you feel it? Of course you can. You don't have blood anymore. You just have power. It runs through you like a trickle of fire, a burning and itching that you can never scratch.

Well, I shouldn't say never. I got to move. Eventually. Only took ten years.

Is it everything you'd dreamed it would be? I doubt it. It's rare when what we want most turns out precisely as we pictured it.

If you're wondering, yes, this is exactly how it felt for me all those years, frozen in one pose in the middle of Somber

End. Watching the people of the town go about their lives.
Waiting each day for a small boy to sit at my feet and break
the boredom by telling me stories, sharing his dreams. You
might not have known that I did appreciate that. Sadly,
though, even then I knew things wouldn't end well for you.

But that power you always asked me for? You got it. It's
all yours. You could make it rain gold. You could enslave
entire nations. That is, if you could move. I guess that's the
price you pay for everything you want.

Thank you, Guntram. I never got to say that. Thank
you. The Nachtfrau created me to guard Somber End, in
case the Leichleben ever broke free from the Hinterlands and
threatened the village. I had a duty to protect. But standing
there all that time . . . Even with a duty, I might have gone
mad without you. You gave me the strength to go on the very
first time you touched me.

Did you know that? I learn the best quality of everyone
who touches me. From you, I got drive and determination.
Did you even know that was your best quality? You were
probably too busy dreaming of gold and power to realize
you could have attained what you wanted by working for it,
instead of expecting it to be handed to you.

But from Alphonsus . . . I got his heart. Literally and fig-
uratively. When he touched me, I understood compassion for
the first time. I never knew how much caring for others could
move you. Again, literally and figuratively. When he needed

me the most, I was able to move and help him. Because I was compassionate.

I hope, Guntram Steinherz, that someday, someone will need you that badly. I hope someone touches you and fills you with the very best of them. Maybe it will be enough to allow you to move again.

Maybe.

39

Death of a Hierophant

Esme pressed her hands to the bleeding hole in her stomach as Aharon and his people grabbed makeshift weapons to face off against the stone creature. But before the monster could make another move, a *crack* like a thunderbolt sounded as a battle-axe severed the creature's head from its body. Just behind it, Sabine lifted her axe, prepared to continue fighting, but the stone creature's body crumbled to the ground.

"Sorry about that," the empress said. "One got past us. But I think that's the last—" She gasped as she spotted Esme, bleeding on the ground. "Esme!"

The villagers snapped into action, gathering supplies to treat Esme's wound. But the young Hierophant knew there was nothing any of them could do to help. She'd been run through. In just a few moments, she'd lost so much blood that her own abilities to heal wouldn't be strong enough. She was dying.

As the empress knelt at Esme's side, the Leichleben let out a mournful roar. Two tendrils of shadow and sand slithered out from the creature's center and swirled around Esme. It was trying to console her. A third tendril reached over, plucked a broken teapot from the wreckage of a nearby yurt, and moved it gently toward Esme's wound.

"No," Esme said, holding up her hand. She smiled at the Leichleben. "I appreciate it. But no. The way you heal won't work on a Hierophant."

The Leichleben withdrew its arms and moved away, keening all the while.

The empress laid her hand on Esme's forehead. "Tell me what I can do. Can the Maiden help?"

Esme shook her head weakly. "I can only be healed by magic. It would take another Hierophant. And I'm the last one outside of the North Lands."

"Not quite."

Esme turned in the direction of this new voice. The villagers parted as the Nachtfrau, donned in her cloak of colorful leaves, stepped forward, smiling.

"Mother . . ."

"Shh . . . It's been a while since I've done this. I need to concentrate."

"I know the truth now," Esme said to the Nachtfrau. "I'm so, so sorry."

The Nachtfrau stood over her daughter, closed her eyes, and began drawing sigils. Each cant she spoke came out sounding like music, a lullaby meant to soothe and protect. Glowing symbols rained down on Esme, closing her wound and healing her injury.

The girl's arms flung open, and she pulled her mother in close. She sobbed as she felt the older woman's fingers run through her hair, something the young Hierophant had always wanted.

The Nachtfrau smiled. "So, you're not going to kill me?"

Esme's eyes went blank. "The Collective didn't send me here to kill you. They sent me here, hoping *you* would kill *me*."

The Nachtfrau nodded sadly. "It was the only way they could see to lift the curse that bound them. The curse you never knew you placed. I can't believe they thought I'd ever do anything to harm you."

"Please explain." Sabine looked from Hierophant to Hierophant.

"Several years ago, Your Majesty," the Nachtfrau said, "the Hierophant Collective—with the agreement of the Hierophant populace—began experimenting with ways to create life using magic. A practice that was strictly forbidden. They built this city and made several secret attempts to forge creatures they could hold complete control over. There were many failures, poor, pitiful beings that they set loose in the Hinterlands. The Collective abandoned these creations. Because they weren't perfect.

"Then they created the Leichleben. It was closer to what they wanted. It was something they could imagine turning into a soldier. Something they could use to overthrow the empire. But that's when I discovered what they were doing. The Collective had been hiding their actions from me, knowing that I wouldn't approve. I confronted them, threatening to expose their plans to you and your wife. We fought. And in the end, they fled."

Sabine looked impressed. "You stood up to the entire Collective on your own?"

The Nachtfrau nodded. "I had just given birth." She stroked Esme's cheek. "I didn't want my daughter to grow up thinking I'd turned away from doing what was right.

"I hid my pregnancy from the Collective. My husband and I had married in secret. And when the Hierophants fled, I begged my husband to go with them and to take Esme along. I couldn't risk them being harmed if the Collective attacked me."

"And," Esme added, "with me living among the Hierophants, you'd have a way to spy on them."

"Yes. But my husband knew it would only be a matter of time before the Collective realized she was my daughter. When that happened, they'd have killed her without a second thought."

Esme took over. "So my father came up with a plan. When I was just barely able to talk, he taught me how to cast a binding spell that forced the Hierophants to stay in one place. There are only two ways to end a spell: the caster can end it on their own, or . . . the caster can be killed by a blood relative. And if the Collective killed me, the curse would go on forever and they'd never be able to leave the North Lands."

"But if they knew you had cast the binding spell," Sabine asked, "why not just ask you to end it?"

"Because I would have figured it out. I would have realized the spell was the only thing keeping me alive. No, the only way for them to end the curse was to have my mother kill me.

"So they trained me to be her assassin. They filled my head with lies about her, told me that she had cast the curse, and the only way to save the Hierophants would be to kill her. They guessed that my mother would defend herself when I showed up."

The sorceress nodded. "I'm sure it gave the Collective

great pleasure to know that I was watching as they turned my own daughter's heart against me. But they never succeeded in turning me against her."

"You should have come to me," Sabine told the Nachtfrau. "You allowed your name to be slandered in all Rheinvelt when you acted only to save the empire. If you had come to me, I would have believed you."

The Nachtfrau bowed her head. "I appreciate that, Your Majesty. But it wasn't possible. I had to act swiftly to protect Rheinvelt from what the Hierophants left behind. I created binding sigils in the canyons of the Hinterlands to prevent the Leichleben and the Collective's other creations from leaving. And I created the Onyx Maiden and sent her to Somber End to protect the village, should the Leichleben ever escape the Hinterlands. The Balance—the consequences of the spells a Hierophant casts—prevented me from discussing what I'd learned with anyone."

The empress narrowed her eyes. "But you're telling me now."

The Nachtfrau put her arm around her daughter. "That's because it doesn't matter anymore."

"What do you mean?" Esme asked.

"Remember what I told you when we first met?"

"You said you could never leave the Hexen Woods because it would kill you. I thought that was a lie."

"My child . . . I have *never* lied to you."

The Nachtfrau fell to her knees. Immediately, Sabine and Esme swooped in and helped lay her on the ground.

"No!" Esme shouted. "No, I'll get you back to the Hexen Woods. You'll be safe there." She began tracing sigils above her head. She didn't care if she glowed for a year. She would get her mother back to the Hexen Woods, where she could live and . . .

The Nachtfrau gently took her daughter's hands in her own and pulled them to her chest. "Esme, it's too late for me. I knew what leaving the woods would do. And I'd make that sacrifice a thousand times over to save you."

Sacrifice?

Once more, a new truth blossomed in Esme's mind. "This is what the rhyme meant. You said the Collective had turned my heart against you. Alphonsus was never the counterclockwise heart. It's me. It's always been me."

The Nachtfrau nodded. "He needed to believe it was him. That was how he found the courage to do what he needed to do. He's got such a strong heart, that boy. I'm only sorry he couldn't save poor Guntram too."

"This was all you. The Maiden, the clock . . . *You* made it all happen."

"Not exactly. My visions of the future were weak. I knew what might happen. And I knew what I had to do so things would end well. I knew the two of you would cross paths someday. And that you'd help each other. And learn from each other. And I knew what I'd do . . . to save you."

Esme's threw herself onto her mother. It wasn't fair! They'd only just found each other. Her mother was all she had left. The sorceress laid an arm across her daughter's shoulders and comforted as best she could.

The empress rose and lifted her arms toward the villagers. "Leave them." She cleared the area until only Esme and the Nachtfrau remained.

Esme sniffed. "No, I can do this. I can heal you."

"Esme, you will do many wondrous things in your life. You have a talent for magic unlike any other Hierophant. More than that, you are a strong, smart young woman who doesn't need magic. Always be that person first. Be that person now. Just stay with me."

The Nachtfrau pulled her daughter close and whispered in her ear. Esme closed her eyes and held her mother. Together, they sang lullabies. They told each other secrets. They both silently wished to turn the clocks back and regain all the time they'd lost. But there were no more backward-running clocks. Not anymore.

Nearby, the Onyx Maiden watched from behind a silver spire. She bowed her head as mother and daughter wept. Her purpose fulfilled, the Maiden set down her flail. Slowly, the dark color of the onyx bled away until the statue was completely clear. No one noticed as the Maiden silently broke apart and dissolved into a pile of sparkling white sand.

Esme rocked her mother gently, back and forth, back and forth. And when she opened her eyes again, she found herself holding only a handful of leaves, patches of caramel-colored fox fur, and the infinitum box.

40

The Fear Within

It was the warmest summer night ever on record when the caravan of Geist refugees, led by Empress Sabine, Prince Alphonsus, and Esme Faust, reached the borders of Rheinvelt. Days of marching across the Hinterlands had left them all exhausted, but everyone found the energy to cross into Somber End, knowing that it meant no longer having to sleep on the ground.

Alphonsus took a deep breath, allowing the scent of pine trees to fill his lungs. He'd missed it. Since running from the empire, he'd convinced himself he'd never live to see his homeland again. He was glad to be wrong.

There was much to do. The empress had promised the citizens of Geist sanctuary in her realm. She swore to find land and homes for everyone. But Alphonsus wondered if it would ever be as easy as that. Even though night had fallen, their arrival had woken the people of Somber End. As Sabine led the party through the streets, shutters opened and curtains twitched as prying eyes peered out at the strange visitors. The prince wondered if all they saw were people with rakes for arms and wheels for feet. And did they still see him as a vessel of the Maiden's evil?

"Ignore them." Esme appeared at the prince's side and whispered in his ear. By way of example, she snapped her head around and met the eye of a flat-nosed man who had opened his door to peek out. He slammed it shut as soon as Esme caught him.

Alphonsus nodded. *They fear what they don't understand*, he told himself. He could still feel his own fear burble inside, waiting for a chance to seize control. But he knew now he'd never let those feelings take over again.

"I never thanked you for enchanting that stone," Alphonsus said. "It worked perfectly. Guntram touched it, and it brought back a memory. The spell you cast made it so I was able to watch. He had a terrible life, Esme. I wish I'd understood that."

"Having a terrible life is no excuse for the things he did."

"I just wish I could have helped."

In the town square, where a pile of white dust that used

to be a plinth served as the only evidence of the Maiden's presence, the empress spoke in hushed tones with the burgermeister. One by one, members of the village constabulary arrived to escort the refugees. They would be staying. All on the orders of the empress. Those who chose to be suspicious of these new people, who were so unlike them, would need to get past those feelings very quickly.

Esme scribbled a single symbol in the air and spoke its cant. Alphonsus watched as the sigil glowed, then faded away.

"What was that?" the prince asked.

"I ended the curse on the Hierophants. They're no longer confined to the North Lands. They're free to keep running away."

Alphonsus gaped. "Aren't you afraid they'll come after you?"

"When they find the curse lifted, they'll assume their plan worked and that I'm dead. They'll keep running because they'll think my *mother* is after them."

The prince shook his head in amazement. "They spent a lifetime lying to you. They tried to make your mother kill you. You could have just let them all freeze to death."

"I know. Your stupid compassion must be contagious."

As the crowd of refugees thinned, Sabine joined her son and the young Hierophant.

"Esme," the empress said, "you and your mother have done the empire a great service. Are you sure I can't convince you to stay with us? As an empress, I wish to thank you. As a parent . . . I worry."

Alphonsus gave Esme a pleading look. She had no family. She couldn't return to the Hierophants. He hated the idea of his new friend being alone.

But Esme had made up her mind. "Someone has to watch over the Leichleben. He was created by the Hierophants. I feel like he's my responsibility. And he's so, so lonely. Plus, he's stuck in the Hinterlands now. When Mother died, the spells she cast to bind him to the Hinterlands became permanent. He needs someone. We can take care of each other."

The empress did not look convinced. Alphonsus could see in her eyes that she was preparing to insist that Esme stay. But the prince had learned there was little anyone could say or do to change the young Hierophant's mind.

"She can visit, Mother," Alphonsus chided.

Esme held up her hand in an oath. "And I will. Often."

"We'll just have to find a dark room in the dungeon so she can glow for a couple days." Alphonsus laughed as Esme—smiling sincerely for maybe the first time since he'd met her—slapped his shoulder.

Sabine bent over and kissed Esme on the forehead.

"Take care, my child. Make sure you let us know you're well. Mothers worry."

The empress went to oversee the housing of the remaining refugees. Alphonsus and Esme stood, staring awkwardly at each other in the moonlight. Neither wanted to say goodbye.

"Before my mother died," Esme said, "she wanted me to apologize to you."

"For what?"

"She's the one who put you in the walls of the palace as a baby. She found you in what was left of the refugee village after the Leichleben's attack and sent you to safety. She had been trying to send you directly to the throne room, knowing the imperial family would take care of you. But . . . she missed."

"Why just me? Why didn't she rescue anyone else?"

"I don't know. Maybe the visions she'd had told her you were important and needed to be protected. Maybe something else stopped her from rescuing anyone else. We might never know."

"The rhyme on the bassinet. She wrote it, didn't she?"

Esme nodded. "But I don't know how she did that either. Seeing the future is supposed to be impossible." She pulled the infinitum box from her pouch and held it to the light. "I have a feeling there's a lot more to this than my mother told me. I think she filled it with stories of her life, the secrets of her magic . . . Everything she'd always wanted to tell me. Maybe it has the answers to the things we haven't figured out yet."

"So you've decided you like who you are with magic more than who you are without?"

"I've decided I'm not two different people. There isn't magic me and nonmagic me. It might just take some time to figure out how that works."

Alphonsus opened his arms. "May I hug you?"

Esme smiled. "Thank you for asking. No, you may not. Compassion is hard enough. I don't know when or if I'll ever enjoy hugging."

The prince laughed. Instead, he settled for a bow deep at the waist. His friend returned the gesture.

Esme stepped back, waved goodbye, then drew the sigils that whisked her away in a flash of golden light, back to the Hinterlands and the Leichleben. Alphonsus took three steps toward his mother and realized he was missing Esme already.

Life wasn't easy for Alphonsus over the next few months. Many still put distance between themselves and the prince. He could feel their eyes boring through his tunic as if searching for his clock. But he always smiled. He always showed he was still the same prince they'd always known. Over time, some began to accept that.

The ticking in his clock had returned to normal. *Brrda-tick! Brrda-tick!* He no longer worried about portents or omens. He loved his clock. He met with Aharon regularly to hear stories of his birth parents. They were good people. He hoped they would have loved who he had become.

Every night, Alphonsus climbed the stairs of the tallest tower in the palace. He lit two lanterns—one green, one blue—and hung them for all to see. From that day on, the light of the royal standards in the tower became a symbol to one and all. Those beacons told everyone that all was well within the borders of Rheinvelt.

And each night, the prince would aim his spyglass to the west. Just on the horizon over the Hinterlands, he saw two sigils—one green, one blue—burst into the sky and twinkle before fading to stardust.

Which meant to him that all was well *everywhere*.

Acknowledgments

This story has lived in my heart for a very long time. Putting it on paper was a trying and often difficult process. I am greatly indebted to my editor, Krestyna Lypen, and the entire team at Algonquin Young Readers for their unflagging support through all the false starts, and bits of wisdom that shone like gems in the dark to help me find my way.

Thanks to the McKnight Foundation, whose support in the form of a McKnight Artist Fellowship for Writers gave me the opportunity to do a dream writing retreat in a Scottish castle, where I worked on this book.

Thanks also to the Loft Literary Center and Bao Phi for administering the McKnight Fellowship, and special thanks to Kate Messner, who judged it.

Sending love to all the other Kindling Words West attendees who joined me in that Scottish castle for a week. Such a caring and generous group of writers. I'm sorry I ate all the haggis.

Many thanks to Mark Schroeder, who read an early draft of the book's first third and then kept asking when he could read the rest. (Is now okay, Mark?)

Thanks to my agent, Robert Guinsler, for advocating for me when my brain was incapable of doing it. It's been good having you on my side.

And, always, all love and thanks to my husband, Benj Farrey-Latz, who gave up a lot so I could have time to write. I owe you so much.